RETURN TO
BONE TREE HILL

RETURN TO
BONE TREE HILL

Kristin Butcher

thistledown press

Thistledown Press Ltd.
633 Main Street, Saskatoon, SK   S7H 0J8
www.thistledownpress.com

Library and Archives Canada Cataloguing in Publication

Butcher, Kristin
Return to Bone Tree Hill / Kristin Butcher.

ISBN 978-1-897235-58-4

I. Title.

PS8553.U6972 R48 2009   jC813'.54   C2009-900758-4

Cover photograph by Sam Javanrouh
Cover and book design by Jackie Forrie
Printed and bound in Canada

10 9 8 7 6 5 4 3 2 1

Canada Council   Conseil des Arts
for the Arts   du Canada

SASKATCHEWAN
ARTS BOARD

Canadian   Patrimoine
Heritage   canadien

Thistledown Press gratefully acknowledges the financial assistance of the Canada Council for the Arts, the Saskatchewan Arts Board, and the Government of Canada through the Book Publishing Industry Development Program for its publishing program.

Acknowledgements

I would like to thank my River Writers group for reading the first draft of the manuscript and for providing me with much-appreciated feedback. I would also like to thank my editor, Rod MacIntyre, for his insight and direction in helping me find all the story's hidden nuggets.

To Rob, who believes in dreams and me

The Dream

The dream is always the same. I've had it so often, it's burned into my brain — flashes of action that jump from scene to scene like clips in a movie trailer.

It begins harmlessly enough — pleasantly even — with Jilly and me playing on Bone Tree Hill. It's August. I can tell by the height of the grass — the colour of it too. The summer sun has bleached it nearly white. It waves in the breeze and rustles as we run through it. I've just turned twelve. I'm wearing the new blue and yellow striped top my grandmother gave me. I'm standing under the tree — arms stretched wide, face turned to the sky — twirling in circles. I'm thinking how wonderfully dizzy I'm getting and wondering if it's possible to de-dizzy myself by twirling the other way, when I hear a wobbly, high-pitched Tarzan call. I look around just in time to see Jilly swoop from the tree on the rope swing. She's coming straight at me. Too dizzy to run, I drop to the ground. At the same time, Jilly jumps, landing on top of me, and we both end up rolling in the grass, laughing.

Then the scene changes, and there are three of us — Jilly, me, and Amanda McCreedy. Amanda moved to our school in grade five, and because she lives next door to Jilly, she hangs out with us a lot. But it's a different day than in the first scene of my dream; it's cloudy and I'm wearing a sweatshirt instead of my striped top. I know it's the same summer though, because the acorns ripened early that year and the three of us are gathering the fallen ones and piling them into a small mountain at the base of the tree.

Then the scene changes again. Now we are crouched behind the oak tree with the mound of nuts we've collected, desperately trying not to laugh at what we're about to do. It's a lost cause. Though our hands are clamped tightly over our mouths, our giggles keep squirting out between our fingers. Jilly peeks around the massive tree trunk and then quickly pulls her head in again.

"He's coming!" she hisses. "Get ready."

We all grab handfuls of acorns. Jilly stuffs so many into her pockets, her shorts nearly fall off when she stands up.

The 'he' she is referring to is Charlie Castle. He's a big kid with a voice to match, and he's yelling at the top of his lungs as he races across the field separating Bone Tree Hill from the Gunderson farm where he lives.

"Where is everybody?" he hollers into the August afternoon.

Amanda, Jilly, and I stay out of sight, hugging the tree and holding our breath as we wait for Charlie to get closer. When his head appears above the top of the hill, he hollers again. Then he scans the grass and squints up into the branches of the tree. Seeing no one, he frowns, and for a second we think he's going to turn around and head back down the hill. But he doesn't, and when his big lumbering body finally comes into full view, we leap from our hiding place.

Charlie isn't the brightest of kids, and it takes a few seconds for him to figure out what's going on. At first he just stands there, rooted to the ground like a fence-post as we pummel him with acorns. It isn't until one of them glances off his shoulder and grazes his cheek that he finally comes to life.

It's like waking a sleeping giant. One second he's a statue, and the next he's bellowing like a wounded elephant and thundering through the grass after us. Around the tree, into the gully, through bushes and over rocks, back up the hill, zigging this way, zagging that, the four of us run — Charlie roaring with rage and Amanda, Jilly, and me screaming in glorious terror.

Then the scene changes again — for the last time. It's evening on Bone Tree Hill and though the sun still clings to the mountains, the warmth has drained out of the day. I have goose bumps on my arms, but at the same time my face feels hot. Jilly isn't there. It's just Amanda and me lying on our backs in the gully, watching the clouds sculpt themselves into flowers and puppies, ballerinas and bicycles, rocking chairs, and flying fish.

"It's getting late," I say, propping myself on an elbow. "I have to get home."

"Yeah, me too," Amanda sighs and starts to push herself up.

Then we hear a voice. It's coming from the hill. Instantly curious, we sink back to the ground, crawl over to a wild rosebush, and peek through its leaves.

Amanda nudges me and nods toward the oak tree.

Charlie's there. He has a shovel in one hand and some sort of tin box in the other, and he's arguing with the tree. His back is to us and he's muttering, so we can't catch what he's saying, but from the tone of his voice and his agitated movements, it's obvious he's upset. As we watch, he sets the box on the ground and starts to dig. Actually, he isn't digging so much as using the shovel's blade to cut into the earth. After a while he leans the shovel against the tree, kneels down, and peels away a small square of sod. He scoops away some of the exposed dirt to create a hole, and into this he lowers the tin box. Then he replaces the sod.

That's when Amanda sneezes.

Instantly Charlie wheels around and peers into the gully. If we stay put, he might not see us, but instead we panic and start to run. So, of course, Charlie runs after us. It's the same old game. Get Charlie mad and then run like heck.

This time though, it's different. I can tell right away. For one thing, my legs are like lead weights, and no matter how much my brain tells them to hurry, they don't want to move. The other difference is Charlie. It's always easy to get under his skin, but it's also pretty easy to outrun him, until eventually he gets tired or frustrated — and gives up the chase. Not this time though. This time Charlie is crazy mad, and I seriously begin to worry what he might do if he catches us.

He charges down the hill at full speed, swinging the shovel in the air and bellowing like a Viking. His face is purple, as if every drop of blood in his body has been rerouted to his head and it's throbbing with the task of pumping it. Or maybe that's my head. I've suddenly developed a ferocious headache.

Normally Charlie would chase both Amanda and me, but this time he focuses all his efforts on her. No matter which way she turns, he dogs her. Little by little, he's gaining ground, and when she stumbles over a loose rock and goes sprawling, it's all over. He should pounce, but for some reason he hurls the shovel, and it flies through the air like a javelin, missing Amanda by a hair and clattering onto a big rock. Amanda doesn't waste a second getting back onto her feet, but Charlie is too close to elude any longer, and in four strides he has her. He grabs her shoulders and begins shaking her so hard I'm sure her head is going to snap off.

"Let her go, Charlie!" I scream, though I can barely hear myself over the hammering in my head. "You're hurting her, Charlie! Let her go!"

But Charlie is beyond hearing.

I have to do something. But what? I'm certainly not strong enough to pull Charlie away.

Then I remember the shovel. If I threaten Charlie with it, he might let Amanda go. But first I have to get it, which is easier said than done since my body is still stuck in slow motion. It seems to take forever to make my way across the grass. Finally though, my fingers curl around the handle of the shovel, and swinging it into the air, I return.

"Charlie!" I scream and then gasp as a searing pain scorches the back of my eyes, setting off orange and white sparks.

I don't know how long they last, but when they clear and I can see again, Charlie is lying on the ground at my feet. He isn't moving. He's just staring at me with empty eyes. His skin is sickly white, and his hair is matted with blood.

Another searing pain; more sparks.

That's when the dream ends and my body jerks me awake. Every time.

One

I lowered myself to the ground, drew my knees up under my chin, and wrapped my arms around my legs. Then slowly releasing my breath, I looked around.

The bank I was sitting on slid gradually into a shallow gorge littered with clumps of bush, spindly trees, and a rocky stream bed choked dry after a rainless summer. On the far side rose another bank, higher and more imposing than the one I was on, and my gaze moved irresistibly to it.

Bone Tree Hill — that's what we kids had called it, though for the moment I couldn't think why. There were no bones there, just a large rolling hill, barren except for a single oak tree and sun-bleached stalks of rye grass waving their long spears like vigilant sentries. The soldier grasses came and went in an endless parade of seasons, but the oak tree had been there forever. It was the most magnificent tree I had ever seen — as wide as it was tall — branches splayed like outstretched fingers, holding the surrounding countryside close. What it couldn't touch, it watched. From its lofty lookout on top of the hill, the tree saw all — and knew even more.

For several minutes, I watched it watching me. Would it remember? It had been six years. I'd changed. No more headstrong tomboy scampering through its branches, plucking acorns and pelting them at unsuspecting victims below. I was eighteen now and in a few more weeks I'd be heading off to university. The tree couldn't possibly remember me now. On the other hand, how could it forget?

"Jessica! *Jess!*" From a distance I heard someone calling my name, and I turned to see Jilly waving madly as she hurried up the trail.

I waved back and stood up.

"I phoned your grandmother's house as soon as I got off work," she shouted up to me. "She said you'd gone for a walk. I knew you'd come here. You're barely in town two hours, and — *zing!* — you shoot straight for the hill."

I smiled and waved again. Considering the hill was the reason I was visiting Victoria, I thought I'd done well to stay away as long as I had. I watched Jilly's long, sure strides cut the distance between us.

"How *are* you?" she demanded the second she reached the top. And then she hurled herself at me.

Six years hadn't changed Jilly a bit. She was as electric as ever — still a bone rack too, and though I returned her hug, I was careful not to squeeze too hard. I didn't want to break her on the very first day.

"Just look at you!" she gushed before I could open my mouth. "You're gorgeous. And you have boobs! Are they real?" She jabbed a finger into one of them.

"Jilly!" I protested, pushing her hand away. But I couldn't help laughing. It was such a Jilly thing to do.

"What?" she blinked innocently. "You were always so paranoid you were never going to grow those things. I was just checking to see if you really had." She threw back her shoulders, pulled her tee shirt tight, and eyed her own chest — what there was of it. "Hmm," she said. "It looks like I'm the one who should

14

have been worrying." Then she shrugged. "Oh, well, what would I do with hooters anyway? They'd just get in the way when I'm running. I'd probably smack myself in the eye or something."

I threw my arms around her again. "Oh, Jilly," I laughed, "you're crazy," but a wave of relief washed over me. I hadn't realized until that second how much I was counting on that craziness to keep me sane.

"Come on," she said, hooking her arm through mine and starting back down the trail. "Mom is dying to see you."

Jilly Carlisle and I had found each other the first day of kindergarten, and after that we'd become inseparable. If Jilly wasn't at my house, I was at hers — usually in the kitchen.

As far as kitchens went, the Carlisles' was pretty basic — nothing trendy or state-of-the-art — just a big old kitchen in a big old house. It didn't even have a dishwasher. The cupboards were white enamel, except where years of wear had taken the paint back to bare wood. The floor was a checkerboard of faded red and white tiles. The walls were tea kettle wallpaper.

The heart of the kitchen was the old plank table. Large enough to accommodate all six Carlisles twice, it ran the entire length of the room. Chairs flanked both sides, but for some reason they always seemed to be full, if not with actual Carlisles, then with the assorted items that decorated their lives. I never went to visit that I didn't have to move a hat or two, the cat, a pile of clean laundry, a toy, some sort of tool, or a stack of books before I could sit down. There was always an accumulation of things *on* the table too — newspapers, coffee cups, potted plants, Mrs. Carlisle's sewing machine, or — if you showed up at lunchtime, which I got very good at doing — plates of sandwiches and cookies. You'd never find a photo of the Carlisles' kitchen in any decorating book, but if there was a magazine about the rooms families actually lived in, their kitchen would be on the cover.

As soon as Jilly yanked open the screen door, a swarm of wonderful smells rushed out to greet us — soap, furniture polish, yeast, cinnamon, and fresh-squeezed lemon. Then Mrs. Carlisle burst through the door too, launching herself at me just as Jilly had done.

It never ceased to amaze me how all the Carlisles could be so skinny. Considering the way they loved to eat, they should have tipped the scale at three hundred pounds apiece. Instead, they looked like the poster family for a starving Third World country. If you stuck them all together, you still wouldn't have had a fat person.

Despite Mrs. Carlisle's bony frame, she was surprisingly strong, and her ferocious hug momentarily took my breath away.

"Jessica, Jessica, Jessica." She finally loosened her hold and stepped back to examine me at arms' length. "You're all grown up!"

"You thought she was going to stay twelve forever?" Jilly said, earning herself a swat on the behind.

"Don't be cheeky," her mother clucked, shooing us both into the kitchen. "Come and sit down, Jessica, and catch me up on things. Jilly shares the news in your emails, but emails only say so much." As she ushered me into a chair, she waved Jilly toward the counter. "Bring over that plate of cinnamon buns, love. And fetch some glasses and the pitcher of lemonade from the fridge."

"Now," Mrs. Carlisle said, her eyes dancing as she slid into the chair across from me, "Tell me everything that's been happening. And don't leave out a single detail."

I took a deep breath. Six years was a long time. It was hard to know where to start. "Well," I began tentatively, "you know about Australia, of course."

We'd moved there when I was twelve; my father had taken a position at the big mineral research centre in Adelaide. He'd said it was a geologist's dream job and couldn't pack his bags fast enough. Mom had been excited too. It was just my brother and me who'd balked at the idea. I didn't want to leave my friends, and Sean didn't want to leave his baseball team. But Mom said I'd make new friends, and Dad said there was baseball in Australia too. So that was the end of the protest.

"For a while you had an accent," Jilly said, dropping a huge cinnamon bun onto her plate and noisily sucking the stickiness from her fingers. "All your *a*'s sounded like *i*'s — *g'die* and like that. Since you've been back in Canada you're talking normal again, but for a while there I thought you'd turned into a regular Aussie."

I rolled my eyes and snorted. "As if! Down there I was constantly getting teased about my Canadian accent."

"Did you like Australia?" Mrs. Carlisle asked.

I nodded and took a sip of lemonade. "Yeah, I did, and that's fairly amazing considering how much I didn't want to go. But once I got over being homesick, it was great."

"I still have all your postcards and emails," Jilly said. "And the souvenirs you sent too." She started counting items off on her fingers "The koala bear key ring, the boomerang, the sand from some beach you went to, that piece of amber with the insect trapped inside — "

"That was courtesy of my dad," I interrupted, reaching for a cinnamon bun.

"I figured as much," she nodded. "Anyway, I still have it. I have it all. And I do mean *all*. You sent me enough stuff to open an Australian gift shop right here in Victoria." Suddenly she sat up straighter, and you could see the wheels in her head starting to spin. "Hmm," she murmured thoughtfully, "that's not a bad idea."

Mrs. Carlisle clucked her tongue and shook her head. Then she turned back to me. "So when exactly did you return to Canada? I'm sure Jilly's told me, but I can't remember."

"Almost a year ago."

She sighed. "But why Calgary? For some reason I thought your family would come back here."

"The Stampede, of course," Jilly mumbled through a mouthful of cinnamon bun.

Mrs. Carlisle raised an eyebrow. "Brought out your best manners for Jessica's return, I see."

Jilly took another huge bite and grinned.

I grinned too. This was like old times — sitting at the Carlisles' kitchen table, listening to Jilly and her mom banter back and forth.

"The Stampede *is* great, Jilly," I told her, "but that's not why we moved to Calgary. It was because of my dad's work — again. A friend of his is some kind of head honcho with one of the big oil companies, and when he offered Dad a job, he and Mom decided it was time to come home."

"Obviously Sean didn't agree," Jilly said.

I shrugged and popped a plump raisin into my mouth. "He was pretty much ready to leave home anyway, and since he's already done first year at the University of Adelaide, he decided to stay on. Besides," I rolled my eyes, "he had a girlfriend. Still does, actually. I wouldn't be surprised if he and Mattie end up getting married. They're both working on their degrees right now, but as soon as they're done, I bet you anything wedding bells start ringing."

Jilly waggled her eyebrows at me. "For you and Bryan too?"

I made a face. "Jilly Carlisle, you are such a goof. How the heck do you come up with this stuff? Bryan and I aren't even thinking about getting married. We've barely been dating four months!"

"Four months and three days," Jilly grinned.

My jaw dropped. "Listen to you, Miss Walking Calendar! You'd think Bryan was *your* boyfriend."

"Don't I wish!" Jilly retorted. "I've seen pictures. The guy is totally hot! You should have brought him with you. I'd gladly take him off your hands."

"Don't you think Myles might have a little something to say about that?" Mrs. Carlisle interjected.

"Myles?" I said, leaning into Jilly. "Myles Robinson? You're dating Myles Robinson? You've had a crush on him since grade one!"

Jilly pulled back and frowned. "Don't exaggerate. Once in my life I may have said he was cute, but I've never had a crush on him. And we are *not* dating."

Mrs. Carlisle stood up and started clearing away the table. "What would you call it then?"

"Running," Jilly sniffed. "We run together. We belong to the same running club, so we run together. Gimme a break. I also run with his dad sometimes. Does that mean I have a crush on him too?"

"Have it your way," Mrs. Carlisle sighed, but she didn't sound convinced. Then changing the subject, she asked, "So what brings you back to Victoria, Jessica, and how long will you be staying?"

Suddenly all the fun went out of the afternoon and I shuddered.

"Oh-oh," Jilly said.

"Oh-oh what?" Trying to ignore the uneasiness spreading through me, I made an effort to sound lighthearted.

"You shivered," she replied. "It's 25° outside, and you just shivered. You can't possibly be cold, so you know what that means don't you?"

I didn't answer.

"Someone just walked on your grave."

Two

"Gin," Gran announced, fanning her cards on the table like a seasoned Vegas dealer. "And that's the game. You lose."

"Not again!" I picked up my grandmother's discard and waved it under her nose. "Why couldn't you have thrown this card away before? I've been waiting ages for the ten of hearts." I slapped it back on the pile in disgust.

Gran began gathering the cards together. "It's just not your night, my girl. You've lost five times in a row." Her eyes twinkled devilishly. "Are you sure you know how to play this game?"

"Very funny," I retorted. My grandmother had taught me gin rummy when I was eight, and the two of us had been playing ever since. We'd fallen a bit behind when I'd moved away, but we'd still managed to squeeze a few hands in around sightseeing trips when Gran had visited Australia. Now that I was back in Canada, she'd already been to Calgary twice, so we were quickly making up for lost time.

She slid the deck of cards into its well-worn pack.

"That's it?" I complained. "You're quitting? What are you — a sore winner?"

She chuckled and squinted at her watch. "Jessica, you know I would happily sit here and whoop the pants off you all night — if I could keep my eyes open. But it's almost twelve, and I am exhausted." She eyed me curiously. "Why aren't *you* tired? It's one in the morning Calgary time."

I drummed my fingers on the table top. "I think I'm too wired. You know — excited to be back in Victoria. Maybe I'll get sleepy if I read."

Though I hadn't let on to my grandmother, I *was* tired. I just didn't want to go to sleep, because then I'd have the dream. I knew I would. It had been almost two weeks since the last time, but now that Bone Tree Hill was just down the road and up the trail, I could almost feel the dream waiting for me.

I wasn't planning on going to bed, but in the dark of the bedroom I changed into my pyjamas. Then I padded to the window, pushed it open, and — leaning over the sill — drew the night air deeply into my lungs. It was cool and fresh and chased away my drowsiness. I gazed up at the star-strewn sky and searched for Orion's Belt. That and the two dippers were the only constellations I could ever pick out. Even with a star-to-star diagram, I could never find the others.

I leaned farther out the window and craned to see my old house. Gran said a young family lived there now, but they were away on vacation. When I'd walked past the house earlier in the day, it hadn't looked much different than I remembered. There was a swing set in the backyard and the deck had been painted, but otherwise the place was the same, and it was weird to think I couldn't march up the driveway and push open the front door.

I'd lived the first twelve years of my life in that house, yet I barely recalled moving out of it. I guess that's because of the meningitis. It had hit me just before we left for Australia, and even though the doctor said it was a mild case and I had made a full recovery, I was really sick for a while. According to Mom I was out of my head with fever for days. We even had to postpone our move.

I could feel my eyelids getting heavy, so I blinked a few times, took another gulp of invigorating air, and reached behind me for the bedside lamp. Instantly a puddle of yellow light spilled onto the bed. Pulling the pillows free of the bed cover, I propped them against the headboard and flopped down. Then I grabbed a couple of magazines from the night table and started flipping through them. Glamorous, air-brushed models stared up at me from page after glossy page, but I barely saw them.

I was thinking about the dream.

It was stupid, really. Even awake the dream filled my mind, so what difference should falling asleep make?

But it did make a difference. Awake, I was in control. I might be reliving the dream, but I was doing it within the safety of consciousness. I could be logical. I could rationalize my fears. I could assure myself that the things shown to me while I was asleep weren't real.

But when I was asleep, the balance shifted. Then the dream was in control, and it was impossible to insulate myself against the terror of it.

The first time I'd awoken drenched in sweat, my heart pounding so hard it hurt. But as sleep receded and my brain cleared, common sense took over. There was nothing to be afraid of. What I'd experienced was just a dream — a nightmare for sure — but still a dream.

That was just after we'd moved to Calgary.

Three months later, I had the dream again. I would have thought I'd be immune the second time, but I wasn't. In fact, I was actually more frightened. I'd never had a dream more than once before, so it felt like I was being haunted — or hunted.

Again I reminded myself it was just a dream, but this time I had a harder time believing it. When I had the dream a third time, I really started to worry. I wasn't a psychic. I wasn't a lunatic. I didn't do drugs. Why was this nightmare chasing me? I thought about telling my parents, but it was too horrible to put into words. Besides, what could they say that I didn't already know? The only thing I could do was pray for the dream to stop.

When a couple of months passed without another occurrence, I thought my prayer had been answered. I even started to relax. So when the dream struck again, I felt as if I'd been ambushed. That's when I came to a realization. Until I could figure out what the dream meant, I was going to continue having it.

That's why I came back to Victoria. That's where the answer was. I could feel it in my bones. I'm not saying I wasn't happy to be visiting my grandmother; I was. And Jilly too, of course. But it was the dream that had drawn me back.

The part I couldn't understand was why I'd never had the dream in Australia. It hadn't begun until I returned to Canada. Why? Was it because I was closer to Victoria and Bone Tree Hill, and my conscience was catching up to me?

A shudder ran down my spine, sending the magazines on my lap sliding to the floor.

How could I even think that? It was like admitting my nightmare was more than a dream — admitting that the horror of it could actually have happened.

I shuddered again.

No!

It couldn't have happened. That was just plain stupid. It was crazy! I wasn't a murderer.

Was I?

Damn! If only I could remember. The meningitis had wiped out a whole week of my life. Apparently I'd been really sick, but I had absolutely no memory of any of it. For me, meningitis had been as powerful as a computer virus. Control, Alt, Delete. Memory gone.

All that was left was the dream and a feeling that something was very wrong.

Three

It was a long night. All I could think about was the dream, so every time my mind unclenched enough for me to drift off, my internal security system kicked in and yanked me back to consciousness. By the time morning arrived I was one jangling nerve, and when Gran poked her head into the room to say good morning, I practically leaped off the bed.

I was still on edge when Jilly picked me up after lunch to go to the mall.

"I see you haven't unpacked yet," she said as I dropped woodenly into the passenger seat.

I frowned. "What are you talking about?"

She tugged at the skin beneath her eyes. "The bags. You look like you're packed for a world cruise."

"I didn't sleep very well last night," I grumbled.

"No kidding," Jilly snorted. Then she heaved a dramatic sigh. "Pining for Bryan, were you?"

I sent her a sideways scowl. "Could we just drop the subject?"

Jilly shrugged and turned back to the road. As she drove, I stared out the window, but I wasn't really seeing anything. I was trying to stifle my bad mood. Being a grump wasn't how I wanted to spend my time with Jilly. And besides, I needed to ask her about Charlie Castle, and I couldn't very well do that if we weren't talking.

I trailed behind as Jilly browsed the wall of sport shoes.

"Charlie?" she said absently. "Sure, I remember him. Gunderson foster kid number 102. Or was it 103? Man, those people took in a lot of kids. Never more than one at a time, mind you. What do you think of this one?" She picked up a white runner with fluorescent stripes and held it out to me.

I shrugged. "It's okay I guess — if you want to glow in the dark."

Jilly made a face. "Cute."

"Well, why are you asking me?" I retorted. "I don't know anything about sport shoes. You're the athlete."

Jilly sighed and put the shoe back. "I don't know why I'm even looking. I don't need new runners. It's just that I got paid today, and I feel like I should buy something."

"Then, buy me a Coke," I suggested, steering her out of the store and toward the food court.

As we got our drinks and headed for a table, I tried to think how I could bring Charlie up again without making Jilly suspicious. All I needed to know was if she'd seen him after I moved to Australia. If she had, then I couldn't have killed him. But I couldn't think how to ask the question without telling her about my dream — which I wasn't prepared to do. At least not yet.

As it turned out, she was the one who brought up the subject.

We'd both been quietly sipping our drinks, when out of the blue, Jilly looked up and started to laugh.

"What's so funny?" I said, glancing behind me to see what had tickled her funny bone.

She shook her head. "Oh, nothing. I was just thinking about Charlie."

"What about him?" I tried not to sound too interested.

"I was just thinking how much he suited his name. Charlie Castle. That was him. Big as a castle and just as dumb." She gave her head a shake and laughed again.

"Jilly!" I protested. "That's so mean. Charlie might not have been the smartest person in the world, but he wasn't stupid."

Jilly stopped grinning. "Are we talking about the same Charlie Castle? Big kid who didn't know his own strength? Kinda dozy? Had a real short fuse? I think he was the prototype for *Shrek*."

"Jilly!" I squealed again, though I couldn't hide a smirk. Except for the fact that *Shrek* was green and Charlie wasn't, the comparison was pretty accurate. Nevertheless, I felt compelled to defend him. "Charlie was just very emotional."

Jilly choked on her drink. "Emotional! Are you kidding me? The kid was certifiably psycho! Don't you remember how he used to lose his temper and chase after us like a maniac?"

"Yeah, but who made him lose his temper?"

Jilly leaned across the table. "Just about everybody. That guy had more buttons than the elevator in the Empire State Building. How could you *not* push them?"

"Okay, so he was a little high-strung," I conceded. Then trying to sound casual, I added, "Whatever happened to him, anyway?"

Jilly sat back and took another sip of her drink. "I don't know. He just disappeared."

Beneath the table, my knee started to shake. This was not what I wanted to hear. "What do you mean — he disappeared? Did the Gundersons send him back to social services?"

Jilly shook her head. "Uh-uh. Nothing like that. He just disappeared — I mean literally. *Poof* — gone, vanished. One day he was there. The next day he wasn't. I don't know where he went. Ran away, probably. The police were called in, but I don't think they ever found him. Or — if they did — I never heard about it."

My mouth felt like I'd just eaten a pail of sand. I took a sip of my Coke, but it didn't help. I cleared my throat.

"When was that?"

Jilly started crunching on a piece of ice. "Right when you moved to Australia. That's why I remember. It was the weirdest thing. On Wednesday there was you, me, Amanda, and Charlie, all hanging out on Bone Tree Hill. And on Friday, it was just me and the tree."

I frowned. "What happened to Amanda?"

"Transferred. Well, her dad was transferred. He was in the navy — remember? Well anyway, he got some kind of big promotion, and the whole family packed up and moved to Ottawa." She snapped her fingers. "Just like that."

I nodded, though I didn't much care. I'd never really thought of Amanda as a friend. She'd just been someone who hung around with Jilly and me for a couple of years. The only reason I ever thought about her at all was because of the dream.

If it was a dream. It seemed to be getting more and more real by the second.

Jilly said Charlie had disappeared. And he'd done it when I was moving to Australia. That was the same time as in my dream. Just a coincidence? I wanted to think so, but the knot in my stomach said otherwise. People didn't just disappear. They ran away. They got kidnapped. Or they were murdered.

"Earth to Jess."

As Jilly waved a hand in front of my face, the world came back into focus.

I blinked a couple of times and gave my head a shake. "Sorry."

"Are you okay?" Jilly asked. "You don't look so good. You're kind of white. And you keep fading in and out. Did you and Bryan have a fight or something?"

I shook my head. "No, nothing like that."

"Well, what then? Something's bothering you."

I opened my mouth and then slammed it shut again. I so wanted to tell Jilly about the dream. Holding it inside was turning me into a basket case. But what if it wasn't a dream? What if the horrible things I saw when I was asleep had really happened? What if they were actually memories and I *had* killed Charlie? I could barely make my mind think the thought, let alone say it out loud. My hands started to tremble, and I quickly clasped them together to keep them still.

I shook my head again.

Jilly reached across the table and squeezed my arm.

"Jessica Lawler, don't you clam up on me," she said. "We've been friends for too long."

Suddenly there was a huge lump in my throat and tears stung my eyes.

"Whatever is bugging you, I can help."

I opened my mouth to argue, but Jilly didn't give me the chance.

Hey," she said, "when we were six, didn't I pull out your baby tooth because you were too chicken?"

In spite of my anxiety, I smiled at the memory — one end of a string wound around my tooth, the other tied to the doorknob, and me with my eyes squeezed shut, waiting for Jilly to slam the door.

"And when Dougie Tattersall took off with your Barbie in grade three, didn't I clobber him with my lunch box and get her back?"

I sighed wistfully. "You did."

"And then when you went to Australia, didn't I save my allowance for four whole months so I could buy a Video Cam and talk face to face with you on the computer? And didn't I — "

"Yes, Jilly, you did," I interrupted. "You did all that stuff and a million other things too. You are the best friend a person could ever have."

"*But?* I'm hearing a 'but'."

I lowered my eyes. "But this time there's nothing you can do to help."

She squeezed my arm again, causing me to look up.

"Don't be so sure," she said. "Don't you remember that summer before you left for Australia and we made that really cool fort in the gully below Bone Tree Hill?"

I nodded. "Yeah. So?"

"Well, remember how Charlie tried to wreck it by pushing a huge boulder right into the middle of it?"

I snickered. "I'd forgotten about that. We were so mad at him."

Jilly chuckled. "No kidding. That time — instead of Charlie chasing us — it was us chasing him." She became serious once more. "Anyway, the *point* is that the boulder was huge. You couldn't move it and neither could I. But when we worked together, we rolled it right out of there. It was a piece of cake." She grinned. "This problem you have now — whatever it is — is just another boulder."

When I was a little girl I hated going to bed. Not the bedtime story or the getting tucked in part. That was all good. I even liked the bit where I got to pretend I was blowing out the light. It was what came after the light went out that I dreaded. If I'd just closed my eyes, I probably would have gone to sleep. But instead I stared wide-eyed into the blackness, straining to see my bureau and chair, my window, my toys, my books. But they were gone, and in their place were huge, scary, shadow monsters. They started out in the farthest corners of the room, but as I lay there, trying to make out their shapes, they would begin to float toward my bed until eventually they were hovering right above me. I imagined I could hear their gravelly voices and feel their hot breath on my skin — and that's when I would pull the covers over my head and scream for my mother. Of course the instant she flicked on the light, the monsters disappeared.

That's how it was when I told Jilly my dream. Putting it into words was like switching on the light. Nothing about the dream had changed — I still didn't know what it meant, and I still didn't know if it was just a dream — but suddenly it didn't seem quite so overwhelming. Sharing it with Jilly had made it less scary. Maybe she was right. Maybe it *was* just a boulder.

At any rate, I didn't have the dream that night; in fact, I didn't dream at all, and the next morning I woke up refreshed and amazingly optimistic. The dream was exactly that — a dream. So when Jilly and I headed up to Bone Tree Hill that afternoon, I wasn't even thinking about it.

Standing beside the tree, I spread my arms, turned my face to the sky, and breathed in the day.

Sprawled on the ground beside me, Jilly started to laugh. "You remind me of that *Sound of Music* movie. Aren't you supposed to burst into song or something right about now?"

I glanced down at her and smirked. "You want me to?"

She scrambled to her feet. "Uh — no. I've heard you sing."

"Oh, Jilly," I sighed and dropped my arms. "This place is amazing. I didn't realize how much I missed it until I came back. You are so lucky. You can come up here whenever you want."

Shading her eyes with her hand, Jilly looked around. "It is kind of nice, isn't it? The funny thing is I *don't* come up here. After you moved away, it just didn't feel right anymore." She ran her hand over the rough grey bark of the oak and looked up into its branches. "Besides, I was getting too old for climbing trees."

"Oh, really," I said, planting a foot firmly into a notch on the oak's trunk. "Are you still too old?"

As Jilly watched me, her eyes glittered and her body tensed. A smile tugged at the corners of her mouth. "That depends," she drawled. "Are you?"

I hesitated for only a second before throwing down the dare. "Last one to the crow's nest is a rotten egg." Then I pushed off and started to climb.

The tree was so big it could accommodate several climbers at one time, and Jilly quickly scooted to the other side and heaved herself up. Being more athletic, she was soon in the lead and won the race easily.

"Ooh, what's that smell?" She wrinkled her nose as I heaved myself onto the branch beside her. Then her face cleared and she jibed, "Oh, of course. That would be you — the rotten egg."

"Very funny," I retorted. "You've obviously been practicing." I jabbed an elbow into her bony ribs. "Shove over."

The crow's nest was a sturdy branch with room for three — at least it used to have room for three. But sitting thigh to thigh with Jilly, it didn't seem quite as spacious as I remembered.

The view was still spectacular though. I could see forever in every direction.

I looked south. "It's like time stood still," I murmured, gazing across endless fields of grazing cows and sheep. A grey ribbon road meandered lazily around them, disappearing into a distant forest of firs and cedars. To the west there was nothing but mountains. To the north was a small lake surrounded by a manicured golf course. "It's like I was just up here yesterday," I marvelled. "Everything is the same."

Jilly shrugged. "That's because the area is zoned for agriculture. Except for a couple of new barns," she pointed toward the patchwork of farmers' fields to the east, "you're not going to get a lot of construction."

"I hadn't thought about that," I said, turning to look. "I'm glad though. I would hate for there to be a car lot where there was supposed to be a cornfield. Speaking of cornfields, do the Gundersons — "

But my question was cut short by a violent shooting pain in my head.

Four

I had just been struck by lightning. I was sure of it. It didn't matter that there wasn't a cloud in the sky; only lightning could inflict that much pain. I gasped and pitched forward on the branch. If Jilly hadn't grabbed me, I would have fallen out of the tree.

"Oh my God, Jess! Are you all right?" she cried, gripping me tightly. "What's the matter? What's wrong?"

I closed my eyes to block out the blinding sunlight, but the splotchy blackness that took its place made my head spin. Afraid of losing my balance, I opened my eyes again. In front of me the world was a mosaic of pulsing jagged shards — a stained glass window that someone had shattered and tried to piece back together.

And then an immense wave of nausea washed over me. I leaned forward and threw up.

"Oh, Lord!" Jilly wailed, clutching me tighter than ever. "Oh, God. Whatever you do, Jess, don't faint. I'll never be able to hold you."

"I won't," I croaked, hoping I wasn't lying. The rough bark of the branch was digging into my legs. I focused on that to keep from blacking out.

Little by little, my light-headedness began to fade. My vision cleared. Then the trembling subsided. I started to feel more like me again. I wiped my mouth on the neck of my tee shirt and let out a ragged breath. I patted Jilly's arm. "I'm okay."

"Are you sure?" She eyed me dubiously, only slightly loosening her hold. "You look like the living dead."

"I'm fine," I said, though I didn't feel fine at all. I forced a weak smile. "I just need to get out of this tree."

"Do you think you can?"

I nodded.

During the downward climb, my legs felt wobbly, but I told myself it was mind over matter. All I had to do was reach the ground — then I could lie down and die.

Jilly was at the bottom when I got there, and she gently lowered us both to the grass. I flopped backwards and let my muscles melt. I was never going to move again.

Jilly put a hand on my forehead.

"You don't have a fever," she said. "That's good." But she didn't sound relieved. "You don't think you could be having another meningitis attack, do you? I mean, isn't this how it happened before?" She didn't wait for me to answer. Instead, she leaped to her feet. "You lie still. I'm going for help."

"No," I groaned, pushing myself up on one elbow and squinting against the sunlight. "No, Jilly. Don't. Please. It's not meningitis." I didn't know that for sure, but people didn't usually get meningitis more than once. Then again, most people didn't get it at all.

Jilly looked uncertain. Her body was tensed, and in her head she was already running. Once that message got to her legs, there would be no stopping her.

I forced myself to sit up and hold out my hand. "Sit with me. I just need to rest for a few minutes. Then I'll be fine."

Reluctantly, Jilly dropped down beside me, and we just sat, leaning against each other in the dappled shade of the tree.

After a while she said, "Are you feeling any better?"

I nodded. "Yeah. I'm just really, really tired. I feel like I could sleep for a hundred years."

Jilly screwed up her face. "What happened? One minute you were fine, and the next you were puking your guts out. I don't get it."

I shook my head. "Me neither. Nothing like that has ever happened to me before, except when I had meningitis."

Beside me, I felt Jilly stiffen.

"Relax," I sighed wearily. "It isn't that. Like you said, I don't have a fever, and when I had meningitis I was out of my head for days."

"Well, then, what is it? People don't go around throwing up and passing out for no reason." She paused and her eyes got round as saucers. "You're not pregnant, are you?"

"Jilly!" I protested in spite of my weariness. "Of course I'm not. How could you even think that?"

She cocked one eyebrow. "Don't act so shocked. Unless you're a nun — which I'm pretty sure you're not — it happens."

If I'd been feeling better, I might have blushed. Instead, I said, "I think what happened up in the tree has something to do with my dream."

Jilly's eyes rolled back in her head, and she fell onto the grass. "Not the dream again!" she groaned. "You are obsessed, you know that? All you think about is that dream. You're letting it take over your life."

"What do you expect?" I shouted, even though the effort set my head throbbing again. "*You* try killing somebody night after night and see if you don't become a little obsessed! Do you have any idea how scary this is?"

Jilly sat up again. "You didn't kill him."

"How do you know that?" I snapped back.

"Because you're not the type. You can't even step on a spider."

"I could have done it by accident."

She shook her head.

"Then explain why Charlie disappeared. And explain why I dreamt about killing him before I even knew he was gone. And tell me why, why, *why* I keep having the dream!"

Jilly chewed on her lip. "I can't. I just know you didn't kill him."

"You're just saying that to make me feel better."

"No, I'm not," she argued. "Well, okay, yes, I am, but it's still true. It would have been almost physically impossible for you to kill Charlie. Even if you *had* — which you didn't — you never would have been able to get rid of the body. Charlie was a big guy. You couldn't have moved him. And what about the blood? You said there was a lot of it. Right?"

I nodded.

"So how come the police never found any? And how come they never found Charlie? No blood, no body, no murder. It sounds to me like Charlie isn't dead."

Thank goodness Gran was out when I got home. I didn't want to have to explain my appearance — I looked like I'd been through a war — and I certainly didn't have the energy to make up a story. I dived straight into the shower, then crashed onto my bed and fell into a comatose sleep.

Later, the tantalizing aroma of cooking food brought me back to consciousness. I felt much better, and I knew I should go to the kitchen and help my grandmother with dinner, but every muscle in my body protested when I tried to move, so I just stayed put and used the time to think.

I tried to look at the situation rationally. Charlie had been missing for six years. In my dream, I saw myself killing him, and I saw him covered in blood. Yet the police never found a body *nor* any blood — not even a murder weapon. Maybe Jilly was right — maybe I hadn't killed him. It made sense, but even so, I couldn't quite convince myself he was alive. Not when I kept having the dream. It was simply too real.

And now there was the incident in the tree to consider. I hadn't mentioned it to Jilly — she was worried enough about me almost blacking out — but right after the pain scorched my brain, I saw Charlie — bleeding and dead. It was like watching a movie — the camera shooting the scene from a distance and then zooming in for a close-up. The thing is that this image wasn't part of my dream. I'd never seen it before. So what did it mean? Was I starting to remember? Or was I just trying to forget? If only I knew.

Right after supper, Gran pulled out the deck of cards and waggled it at me.

"Ready for another whooping?" she teased.

"Actually, no. Not tonight, Gran," I said.

Her jaw practically hit the floor. "You don't want to play?" She sounded hurt.

I walked over to the table, pulled out a chair and sat down. Then I looked up at her and grinned. "Of course, I want to play. I just don't want to get whooped." I rapped my knuckles on the table. "Deal." As she sat down, I added, "And no cheating this time."

"You cheeky thing!" she sputtered, giving my wrist a good-natured smack. "I'll have you know I have never cheated at rummy in my life." She made a big show of shuffling the deck. "Of course, playing with you, I've never had to."

"Listen to you!" I hooted, as I watched her deal. "Now who's being cheeky?" I pushed up my sleeves and picked up the cards. Then I chuckled fiendishly. "But it's not going to do you any good, Granny, dearest. Tonight you're goin' down."

Gran and I bantered back and forth like that the whole evening, trying to best each other at wisecracks as well as cards. When we finally called it quits, I was the one with bragging rights. Not by much, mind you, but I was still the winner. And that meant I got to gloat.

"Well, I have to say you are a very gracious loser, Gran," I sighed as she set a cup of tea on the table in front of me. "I guess that's because you've had so much practice."

My grandmother clucked her tongue. "Just wait until I tell your mother how rude you are."

I squeezed a lemon wedge into my tea. "I don't think she'll be surprised."

"Oh?" my grandmother said cautiously. "Why is that?"

I picked up my cup and blew gently on the steamy brew inside. "Because she's always telling me how much like you I am."

I barely had a chance to set my cup down before we both burst out laughing.

"Oh, Jessica, it's so wonderful having you back," Gran patted my hand. "How I wish you lived closer. Evenings like this are a tonic for me."

I smiled. "For me too. But, hey — now that Mom and Dad and I are in Calgary, we'll have lots more of them."

"I suppose," she sighed. "But it will never be the same as when you lived down the road."

I took a sip of tea. "Jilly and I were talking about that this afternoon. She was trying to update me on everything that's happened while I've been gone."

Gran crossed her arms and leaned on the table. "And what did she say?"

"Well, for starters, she told me that Amanda McCreedy's family moved to Ottawa. I can't believe I didn't know that. She also said that Charlie Castle disappeared."

I watched my grandmother for a reaction.

She frowned. "Charlie Castle. The name sounds familiar, but I can't put a face to it."

"Sure you can, Gran," I said. "He was one of the Gundersons' foster children. He moved here the winter before we left for Australia." I stretched out my arms. "Really big kid with dark hair that fell into his eyes. Mostly quiet, except when he got — " I started to say *angry* but changed my mind. "Upset," I finished.

Gran nodded. "Ah, yes. Now I remember him. Such a sad boy. And lonely too, I think. If ever a child needed to be hugged, it was that one."

My grandmother's words stunned me. Hug Charlie? I couldn't picture it. Charlie hug someone else, maybe — hug them until their eyeballs popped. But the other way around? No way. So why had Gran said that? I would have asked, but I didn't want our conversation to drift off-topic.

"Do you remember when he went missing?"

Gran took a sip of her tea. "Vaguely," she replied thoughtfully. "At that time I was more concerned with you being sick. Then, of course, there was the whole business of the move to Australia. But after you left, I did pick up bits of information here and there. Mind you, I can't say how much truth there was to them.

There was a police investigation though. I even had a nice young detective at my door one day."

"Really?" I said. "What did he want?"

"*She*," Gran corrected me. "It was a woman — Detective Celia Norris. She didn't look anything like I imagined a police detective should. And her name was so pretty, it stuck with me. Anyway, mostly, she wanted to find out how well I knew Charlie, if I had seen him recently, and if so — when and where."

"Did the police have any leads?"

"Detective Norris didn't really say, other than there was no evidence of foul play."

"You mean no body or blood or anything like that."

She nodded. "Yes, except that the night your friend went missing, it rained torrents. I remember because that's the same night you went out of your head with fever and had to be rushed to the hospital. Any blood there might have been would have been washed away. Don't get me wrong," she added quickly. "I'm not saying the boy came to a violent end. I'm just saying that if there had been blood, the rain would have done away with it."

"Oh," I said, my optimism faltering. "I didn't know about the rain."

My stomach began to squirm with worry again, and my thoughts started whirring around in my head. Maybe Jilly's theory wasn't so great after all. If the blood could be explained away, maybe the body could too.

Five

The phone rang just after ten the next morning. Gran was out in the yard puttering in her garden, so I answered it. "Hello?"

"Good morning," Jilly's voice rang out cheerfully on the other end of the line. "How's it going?"

"Not bad," I replied, flopping onto a chair. "I thought you had to work today."

"I do. But I'm on my coffee break, so I thought I'd give you a call. How'd you sleep last night? Any *dreams?*"

My stomach started to flip, and I sucked it in as hard as I could to keep it still.

"No," I said. It was the truth. I'd had a horrible sleep — *again!* — but at least I hadn't dreamed. As if on cue, I yawned into the phone. "Sorry," I apologized. "But I stayed up late playing cards with my grandmother." I paused. "I asked her about Charlie."

"And?"

"And she doesn't know anything. She said the police questioned her though. Do you think they talked to Amanda too?" Amanda was the one person who should have been able to answer the questions I couldn't. Unfortunately, she wasn't around to ask.

"I doubt it," Jilly said. "When would they have had the chance? The police didn't know Charlie was missing until the next day, and like I told you, that's when Amanda's family left." She paused. "Don't you think that's kind of strange? Moving away so fast, I mean. Why the big hurry? And why didn't Amanda say anything to us?"

I didn't even have a chance to answer before Jilly gasped into the phone, "Hey, maybe *Amanda* murdered Charlie! She murdered Charlie, ran home and told her parents, they got rid of the body, and then they all got on a plane for Ottawa. What do you think?"

"I don't know what I think," I sighed. Jilly's theory was pretty far-fetched, but then so was my dream. "All I know is that Charlie's disappearance and my dream are connected. Did the police talk to you?"

Jilly sighed. "Yeah, but there wasn't much I could tell them. I hadn't seen Charlie that day."

"What do you mean? Why not?" Jilly and I had hung out with Amanda and Charlie practically every day that summer.

"Because I spent the day at the hospital. Don't you remember?"

"I was getting sick," I reminded her. "I don't remember much of anything."

"Right," Jilly said. "Well, at lunchtime — instead of slicing my sandwich — I sliced myself and spent the rest of the day in the emergency room, waiting to get stitches. I was so upset, I cried the whole time. Not because I'd cut my hand, but because you were moving and I was sure I was never going to see you again."

"Except that I didn't end up moving for another week."

"I didn't know that then though. And besides, you were so sick we didn't get to hang out anyway."

"True," I conceded. I steered the conversation back to Charlie. "My grandmother told me something interesting about the weather the night Charlie disappeared. She said it rained buckets."

"Is that important?"

"Think about it. The rain would have washed the blood away."

"If there was any," Jilly countered. "Like I said before, I think Charlie is still alive. He just doesn't want to be found. But even if he is dead, I don't think you're the one who killed him."

"You make it sound so simple."

"It is!" Jilly shouted into the phone. "You didn't kill Charlie. Why can't you believe that?"

"Because of the dream."

"Dream shmeam," she muttered. "Dreams aren't real. Didn't anybody ever tell you that? If the stuff in dreams really happened, I'd be able to swim from Victoria to Brazil in half an hour — with hungry alligators snapping at my heels."

"This dream is different. It's too real not to have happened. My subconscious is trying to tell me something. I know it is. I can feel it. If I could just remember. Maybe if I — " My voice trailed off.

"Maybe if you what? Oh, never mind," Jilly said in a rush. "You can tell me later. My coffee break is over and my boss is giving me the evil eye. I get off work at three. I'll drive by and pick you up. We can do something."

That's when a thought struck me, and I said, "And I know what."

Though the bulk of their produce was sold in grocery stores, the Gundersons had a roadside stand at the bottom of the long dirt driveway leading to their farm.

Jilly pulled up behind a dusty SUV and shut off the engine.

I climbed out and looked around. I might as well have been looking at an old photograph. Nothing had changed. A wire fence with grey weathered posts flanked the driveway and continued around a field where grazing cows twitched their tails at pesky flies. Beside the road, blackberry bushes humming with drunken yellow jackets climbed the end of a large lean-to vegetable stand. I couldn't begin to count the number of times I'd visited that stand as a kid. It looked exactly the same — even the colour. The red paint was just a little more faded. The inside of the stand was as basic as it could be — a wooden counter and assorted bins and baskets filled with fruit and vegetables.

A girl of about fifteen stood behind the counter, ringing a sale into an ancient cash register.

I nudged Jilly. "Who's that — another Gunderson foster child?"

She shook her head. "After Charlie, the Gundersons didn't take in any more kids." The girl looked up and smiled. Jilly smiled back. "That's Christina Jones. You remember the Joneses. They run the riding stable up the road. Melanie Jones was in our class."

My eyes bugged out, and my mouth dropped open. "That's Melanie's little sister?"

Jilly chuckled. "Uh-huh, except — as you can see — she's not so little anymore."

As Jilly and I made our way toward a barrel piled high with corn, I peered at the people milling around the stall. Even though it had been my idea to come here, I was still nervous.

"I don't see the Gundersons," I murmured.

Jilly shrugged. "They might turn up."

"I hope so," I replied as I rooted around for an ear of corn and ripped back the husk. I stabbed one of the kernels with my nail. Sticky milk squirted back at me. The sweet smell made my mouth water. It had been ages since I'd had a corn feast.

Even so, that wasn't why Jilly and I had come. Not really. Buying corn was just an excuse to talk to the Gundersons. I needed to ask them about Charlie. I needed to find out what they knew about his disappearance.

It wasn't that I thought I was going to solve the mystery. After all, it had been six years, and if the police hadn't been able to figure out what happened to Charlie, there wasn't much chance I was going to. It was just that I thought — I hoped — that the Gundersons might say something to jog my memory. Because I *did* have a memory of that day. I had to have. I'd lived it, so I had to have a memory of it. It was inside me somewhere; I just had to find it.

Jilly glanced at the pile of corn between us. "That should be enough, don't you think?"

I eyed the pile skeptically. "I'm not sure. You're coming for dinner, so that makes one for me and one for Gran. Is ten going to be enough for you?"

Jilly made a face, then scooped up an armful of corn and headed to the counter.

"Looks like somebody's having a corn roast," Christina grinned. "How many do you have?"

"A dozen," I said, slapping a ten-dollar bill onto the counter.

Jilly pushed the money back at me and reached into her pocket. "My treat," she said.

"Forget that," I told her. "You are not paying — not after the millions of meals I've had at your house."

Jilly rolled her eyes. "Right. And in the thirteen years we've known each other, I've never eaten at your place."

I hip-checked her out of the way and once again slid the money toward Christina. She took it and punched in the sale. Then she gave me back my change. "It sounds like you and Jilly are old friends."

I grinned. "Ever since kindergarten." Then I stuck out my hand. "I'm Jessica Lawler. I used to live around here."

Christina shook my hand. "I'm Christina Jones. I live down — "

I nodded. "You're Melanie's sister."

She beamed. "Yeah."

"How long have you been working here?" I asked, buying some time in the hope that the Gundersons would show up.

"This is my first summer." Christina made a face. "The pay's not great, but it beats picking berries."

I glanced at my watch. It was nearly five o'clock. "So what time do you close up?"

"I'm here until six. Then a guy comes in and looks after the stand until nine. That's when Mr. Gunderson shuts things down for the night."

I wasn't going to get to talk to him. Disappointment rounded my shoulders, but somehow I kept the smile on my face. "Well, at least you get your evenings off," I said as cheerfully as I could manage.

"Yes, thank goodness. Otherwise I'd never see my friends." She sighed. "A bunch of us are supposed to be going to a movie tonight, but unless Mr. Gunderson pays me before I leave, I won't be able to go." She lowered her voice and added, "He doesn't always remember when it's payday."

Jilly shrugged. "So just detour up to the house before you head home and remind him."

Christina shook her head. "I can't do that. I'd lose my job. Mr. Gunderson is very strict. He has rules about everything, and he doesn't forgive people who break them."

Jilly frowned. "So what rule would you be breaking by asking for your pay?"

Christina came around the counter and nodded toward the gate. There was a huge sign nailed to it.

"Private property. Absolutely no trespassing," it read.

"There's another one too," Jilly pointed. "Guard dog. Beware."

"The Gundersons never used to have a *No Trespassing* sign on their property, did they?" I asked as Jilly and I sat on my grandmother's deck, shucking corn.

"Not that I can remember," she said.

"So how come they do now?"

She looked at me across the growing pile of corn husks. "Do you think they're hiding something?"

I shook my head. "I have no clue. But I think I need to find out."

Six

After Jilly and I helped Gran with the supper dishes, we headed for Bone Tree Hill. The sun was still shining, but the colour had been sucked from the sky so that now it seemed more grey than blue. The day had cooled off too, so I grabbed a jacket on my way out the door, and Jilly stopped at her car to pick up a sweater.

We hiked along the shoulder of the road until we got to an overgrown trail. That was the turnoff. It started as a dirt track winding through a meadow, but soon it got steeper and the meadow gave way to outcroppings of rock. These gradually ran together until they formed a small mountain. The only breaks were skimpy patches of dry grass and clumps of purple foxglove that somehow managed to grow right out of the rock.

When we reached the top of this first hill and crossed the gully to Bone Tree Hill, I sagged against the trunk of the oak tree and looked back. It was hard to believe I used to make that climb every day — sometimes more than once. I shifted my gaze to the downward slope ahead. Though every bit as steep as the hill we'd just climbed, the ground on this side fell away in grassy waves that tumbled into a thick hedge of honeysuckle and wild rose bushes at the bottom.

The Gunderson farm was beyond that.

Jilly and I jogged down the slope, swerved around the bushes, and skidded to a stop.

"Where did this fence come from?" I said, staring down the line of wooden posts stretching into the distance.

"Beats me," Jilly shrugged, grabbing the wire and shaking it. "Do you see a gate anywhere?"

I walked down the fence line. "No gate," I called back. "But there's another *Private Property — Keep Out* sign."

Jilly came to look. She shook her head. "There's a definite pattern going on here — fences everywhere, a guard dog, and *No Trespassing* signs. Do you think the Gundersons are trying to tell us something?"

"If you mean do I think they're doing this especially for us — no, but on the other hand, they don't exactly have the welcome mat out either."

"Unless it's one of those ones that says, *Go Away*," Jilly grumbled and headed back to the spot where we'd first encountered the fence. She gave it another shake and then — to my surprise — started climbing.

"Hey," I hollered, hurrying after her, "what about the *Keep Out* sign?"

She jumped to the ground on the other side and blinked innocently. "I don't see any sign." Then she grinned and started loping across the field. "So are you coming or what?"

I started to climb the fence and then stopped. "Maybe I should just telephone the Gundersons. What if we run into their guard dog?"

Jilly turned and waved a plastic bag in the air. "No worries. I've got the situation covered."

I pointed to the bag. "What's that?"

She waved it again. "It's the steak your grandmother didn't finish at supper. You know — just in case Poochie's bite is worse than his bark."

Right away, the image of a vicious Doberman Pinscher popped into my head. His teeth were bared and there were strings of spittle dripping from his jaws. A shiver rippled through my body, and I almost fell off the fence. Somehow three ounces of meat didn't seem like much of a defence against ninety pounds of snarling dog. This visit to the Gunderson farm might not be such a good idea after all. Not that I could change my mind. Jilly was already halfway across the field. So I pushed the image of the dog from my head and hurried to catch up.

The field was newly cut, but it hadn't been bailed, so the hay lay in ragged rows on the stubbled ground, and as my feet scissored through them, the stalks scattered like weightless pick-up sticks.

Jilly was waiting for me on the far side of the field. Here the land dipped again, offering a panoramic view of the entire Gunderson farm. The various crops were planted in huge rectangular plots — potatoes, pumpkins, beans, carrots, corn, onions, and cucumbers. Behind these, the farmhouse, barn, and other outbuildings were flanked by an orchard of fruit trees.

I stared hard at the house — tiny from this distance — trying to catch a glimpse of the Gundersons or their dog, but the only sign of life was a lone chicken strutting along the dirt drive, stopping every few steps to scratch at the ground.

I chewed on my lip. Talking to the Gundersons was proving to be more of a challenge than I'd imagined. In fact, it was beginning to feel like a Herculean task, and if Jilly hadn't been with me, I would have turned around and run for home. Even with her standing beside me, I was still tempted to bolt. Then

I thought about Charlie. I couldn't go through life wondering if he was dead and — if he *was* — wondering if I was the one who had killed him. I grabbed Jilly's hand. "Come on," I said. "Let's get this over with."

Taking the grassy path between the plots of potatoes and corn, we headed for the house. I stayed close to Jilly, keeping one eye peeled for the guard dog. Jilly must have been on the lookout too, because she was totally quiet — not normal behaviour for Jilly — and her eyes were darting around like they were attached to a humming bird. Even so, neither of us saw the dog coming.

We were just nearing the corner of the barn when the most enormous bark I've ever heard erupted out of nowhere. It was so loud, so deep, and so close that Jilly and I both jumped. Then Jilly grabbed my hand and pulled me behind a rain barrel. As far as shields went, it was a pretty pitiful defence; it might slow our attacker for half a second, but that was about all. Just the same, it was comforting to think there was *something* between us and the end of the world.

Glued together like Siamese twins, Jilly and I hugged the wall and waited. The barking continued, but no dog appeared.

Jilly pointed to the barn. "It's in there," she rasped.

"So why doesn't it come out?" I whispered back.

She shook her head. "I don't know. Maybe it's tied up or in a cage or something. I'm going to go look."

I tightened my grip on her arm. "Are you crazy! You'll get mauled to death."

Jilly hesitated for a second, then peeled my fingers from her arm. "If it was loose, it would have been here by now."

She started edging her way past the barrel. Even though I thought she was out of her mind, I was right behind her. The dog continued to bark. Jilly slithered around the corner of the barn and peered into the black cavernous hole beyond the open doors. Then suddenly her body relaxed, she pushed herself away from the wall, and started into the barn.

I latched onto her arm again to pull her back. "Jilly," I wailed, "don't be dumb!"

"It's okay," she said, almost laughing. "This big guy is harmless. Look for yourself."

The barking was as loud as ever, and I peeked cautiously over Jilly's shoulder toward the source — a huge black Labrador Retriever.

"What makes you think he's harmless?" I said, continuing to use Jilly as a shield.

"Look at his tail," she replied, walking into the barn. "Dogs wag their tails when they're happy, not when they're about to attack." She held out her hand.

That's when I realized the dog was chained up. As he strained against his tether, his bark turned into an excited whine, and his tail began wagging harder than ever. He pushed his head into Jilly's outstretched hand, and when she bent to pet him, he waggled his big body against her and smothered her face with doggy kisses.

"Good boy," Jilly crooned, scratching him under the chin. "Good boy. You're not a vicious old guard dog at all, are you? You just want somebody to play with."

"Get off my property or I'll call the police," snapped a voice behind us.

Jilly and I whirled around. Standing in the entrance to the barn was a frizzle-haired, middle-aged woman. She was jabbing a broom at us and glaring daggers, but even so she didn't seem particularly scary. With a bib-apron over her faded print dress and a flour smudge on her cheek, she simply looked like a disgruntled housewife who'd been dragged from her kitchen.

"You heard me." Mrs. Gunderson waved the broomstick at us again. "I said get out. This is private property. Didn't you see the signs?"

Jilly shrugged. "Actually, there were no signs where we were. We climbed the fence over there." She pointed toward Bone Tree Hill.

Mrs. Gunderson didn't seem convinced. In fact, her scowl deepened.

"We're sorry," I apologized, hoping a more humble approach might help the situation. "We thought the fence was to keep the deer out. My grandmother is always complaining about them raiding her garden."

Mrs. Gunderson hesitated. Finally — though she kept the broom trained on us — she growled, "What do you want?"

"We were hoping you could help us." I tried a timid smile.

It had no effect. The woman's eyes narrowed suspiciously. "Help you how?"

I tried another smile. "My name is Jessica Lawler, and I used to live on the other side of the hill. This is my friend, Jilly Carlisle. You probably don't remember us, but when we were kids we used to play with Charlie Castle."

It might have been my imagination, but I could have sworn Mrs. Gunderson flinched.

I waited for her to say something, but when she didn't, I continued. "My family moved away six years ago so I had no idea Charlie had disappeared — until I came back to Victoria, that is. Charlie was my friend — " I faltered, stunned I think by the lie I'd just told. Amanda, Jilly, and I had played with Charlie — that was true enough — but we'd never really been his friends. The realization made me squirm inside my skin. If Charlie had had a friend, he might not have disappeared. "I — I was hoping you could tell me what happened to him,"

I said, pushing aside my feelings of guilt. "I know you might not want to remember that time — I'm sorry if I've made you uncomfortable — but it's important to me. If you could tell me what you know, I'd really appreciate it."

Whether Mrs. Gunderson would have told me anything or not, I'll never know, because just as she opened her mouth, the dog started to bark.

"Blackie!" she scolded him and then glanced over her shoulder toward the dirt driveway.

I followed her gaze and saw a cloud of dust moving up the road.

Mrs. Gunderson's body stiffened. Then she shook the broom at us again. "Go. You don't want my husband to find you here."

"You were — " I began, but she cut me off.

"Didn't you hear me?" Her glance darted towards the road again. "I said, go!" The dust cloud was getting closer. There was a look of desperation on Mrs. Gunderson's face now. She lowered the broom. "Please."

The woman was clearly afraid. I thought about what Christina had told us at the vegetable stand. She'd said Mr. Gunderson wasn't a man you wanted to mess with. I hadn't gotten the information I'd come for, but there was no time to worry about that now. I nudged Jilly. "Come on," I said. "Let's get out of here."

As we took off up through the garden, I looked back. Mrs. Gunderson was scurrying toward the house, away from the old blue pickup truck that had just squeaked to a stop at the top of the driveway. I watched the door open and a wiry man in shirt sleeves, dusty jeans, and a battered fedora step out. It was Mr. Gunderson. If you'd asked me two minutes earlier what he looked like, I wouldn't have been able to tell you, but seeing him again I wondered how I could have forgotten. There was a meanness about him that practically oozed from his pores. He wasn't the kind of man you forgot. And yet I had.

I thought about the last time I had seen Mr. Gunderson. It was that summer I was twelve.

I had come to call on Charlie. He was supposed to meet Amanda, Jilly, and me on Bone Tree Hill right after lunch, but when he didn't show, we decided somebody should go get him. I was elected.

I saw Charlie as soon as I started down the grassy path between the corn and potato fields. He and Mr. Gunderson were standing in front of the barn, and they were arguing. Charlie wanted to go and play, but Mr. Gunderson had other ideas.

"Life is not a free ride," he said, shoving a pitchfork and shovel into Charlie's hands. "The animals need feeding and the barn needs mucking out. So get to it."

Charlie stomped his foot. "My friends are waiting for me!"

Mr. Gunderson raised his voice. "Well, they'll just have to wait a little longer! Get to work!"

"No!" Charlie shouted, throwing down the tools and turning to leave.

Before he could take one step, Mr. Gunderson reached out and smacked him hard across the head. Charlie's ear instantly turned red. So did his face — he was obviously boiling mad — and for a second I thought he was going to hit Mr. Gunderson back.

But he didn't. Good thing too. The scowl on Mr. Gunderson's face was ferocious enough to crack rock. It seemed to me Charlie should cut his losses and be grateful that all he'd received was a sore ear. I guess he thought so too, because without another word, he picked up the shovel and pitchfork and headed into the barn.

As for me, I sneaked back to Bone Tree Hill before anybody saw me.

I shook myself out of the memory and watched Mr. Gunderson move to the back of the truck and lower the tailgate. He was concentrating on whatever he was unloading, so he hadn't noticed me, but I suddenly realized that if he looked up, he'd be staring right at me. Jilly and I had to get off the path. I grabbed her arm and yanked her into the cornfield.

"What the — "

"Shhhh," I hissed, dragging her along the dirt path between the rows of corn. "Just stay low and keep quiet, or Mr. Gunderson will see us. We're going to have to work our way back to the fence through the corn."

"I've always wanted to go through a corn maze," Jilly whispered as we squeezed through row after row of the tall plants, "but I never thought it would be like this. This cornfield is huge. How much farther 'til we get to the end, do you think?" When I didn't answer, she turned around. "Jess?" When I still didn't answer she made her way over to where I was standing. "Jess? Is something wrong?"

I ran my hands over the corn plants on either side of me, but I couldn't feel them. It was like I was inside a foggy dream. "I think I just remembered something," I mumbled, turning my gaze from the corn to Jilly. "I've been here before. In this cornfield. With Charlie. The day he disappeared."

Seven

The flashback in the cornfield wasn't like the one I'd had in the tree. There was no stabbing pain and no image flooding my mind. In a way, I suppose it wasn't a flashback at all. It was more like the shadow of a memory, fuzzy and far away. And yet I knew it was real. It was the same feeling as having a word on the tip of my tongue. It was there; I just couldn't grab hold of it.

As soon as I walked into the cornfield and started pushing through the plants — *zap!* Something hit me. I knew I had been there before — with Charlie. And I knew it had been on the day he'd disappeared. I couldn't actually remember the event; I couldn't picture it in my mind. But that didn't change the fact that I knew it had happened. I would have bet my life on it.

Memories of that day were slowly coming back to me. That's what I wanted — what I'd been hoping for — except that this latest breakthrough came wrapped in a creepy feeling. Whatever had happened in that cornfield, it hadn't been good.

No matter how I tried to push the sense of foreboding away, I couldn't shake it, and during the evening I felt myself sinking into a depression. I tried to be cheerful when my parents telephoned, but they saw through my act. Fortunately, they bought the excuse that I was tired. Bryan, however, was harder to convince. He called a few minutes after my parents, and right away he knew I was irritated. No matter how much I insisted it was because I was tired, he was sure I was upset about something and just wasn't telling him. He was right, of course — I *was* upset, very upset — but I couldn't tell him why, and I couldn't make him believe that the problem wasn't with us, so our conversation ended in an argument. My grandmother was the only one who seemed to accept my excuse without question. She didn't even press me to play cards. Instead she sent me to bed with a cup of tea.

Who knows? Maybe my excuse was actually the truth. Maybe I really was tired, because that night I slept like I'd been drugged and woke up the next morning feeling like a new person — refreshed and optimistic. Before I even got out of bed, I called Bryan. Setting things right between us lifted my spirits even more and — determined to hang onto that feeling — I evicted all thoughts of Charlie from my head.

"Good morning, Gran," I yawned, as I padded to the kitchen and poured myself a glass of juice.

"Good morning," she smiled. "Did you have a good sleep?"

I yawned again and pushed my tousled hair out of my eyes. "Yeah, I did. I had a great sleep. I was out the second my head hit the pillow. I must have been more tired than I thought."

"I'm not surprised. Whatever you and Jilly have been up to, it's certainly been tuckering you out."

I slid onto the chair opposite her and took a sip of juice. "Personally I think it's all the sea air I've been breathing. I'm not used to it anymore."

"Have you and Jilly been to the beach?"

I shook my head. "No, but it doesn't matter. I think the ocean air has been coming to me. Now that you mention it though, a trip to the beach is a super idea. What do you say? Want to make a day of it? We could drive into Sidney this morning and do some shopping — hit all those neat little stores on Beacon Avenue. After that we could have lunch, and then we could take a walk along the beach."

"What about Jilly? Don't you want to spend the day with her?"

I shook my head. "Jilly has to work. And besides, this is something I want to do with you. What do you say?"

Gran grinned. "Why not! But I'm warning you, if these old legs give out halfway down the beach, you're going to have to carry me back."

Sidney is a half-hour drive from my grandmother's house. Though I have always thought of it as part of Victoria, it is actually its own little town — very clean, very quaint, and very picturesque. Our destination was Beacon Avenue, the town's main drag and a shopper's paradise.

Neither Gran nor I had intended to spend any money — our plan was to browse — but the stores were filled with so many amazing bargains that our plans changed when we weren't looking, and before we knew it, we had more bags than we could comfortably carry.

"I think we need to consolidate," I said as I juggled my packages. "Here, Gran. Give me that big bag you have and we'll stick all these smaller ones inside."

"Good idea." She unrolled the top and I shoved the other bags into it. None of them weighed much, so although the big bag was bulky, it wasn't heavy.

"That's better," I said, closing it again. "Where to now?"

Gran pointed across the street. "Tanners, I think. I'm dying to read the new Mary Higgins Clark mystery. I've reserved it at the library, but I'm way down the waiting list. My name probably won't come up for another six months, and there is no way I can wait that long. If it's in Tanners, I'm going to buy it. I've made up my mind," she added vehemently, as if she thought I might try to talk her out of it.

I laughed. "All right then. I'm convinced. Let's go."

Tanner's did have the novel, and Gran did buy it — as well as another book. As for me, I stuck to browsing the magazines and kept my wallet securely zipped inside my purse.

As we hit the street once more, Gran glanced at her watch. "Goodness. It's 12:15 already! I wondered why my stomach was growling."

"Now that you mention it, I'm a little hungry too," I said. I pointed toward the bandstand in the park at the end of the street. "Why don't we head that way? We can eat on the patio of one of the restaurants on the water."

"Sounds like a plan to me," she said, and we started walking again.

But we'd barely gone ten steps, when I pointed to a collectibles shop up ahead.

"Oh look, Gran," I said. "Let's stop in here for a minute. This place might have some of those old cookie cutters Mom likes. It's her birthday next month, and I've been trying to think what to get her. Cookie cutters would be perfect."

A small brass bell tinkled as we pushed open the door. Then the shop swallowed us up. It was long and narrow, composed of a series of small rooms hooked together like railway cars, each one stuffed to the rafters with wonderful curios. The walls were smothered with paintings and wall decorations of every size and description. Tables and bureaus were heaped with silver, glassware, crockery, and linens. Every other thing you could think of was crammed into antique armoires. The shop was so full there was barely room to walk, and treasure hunters had to shuffle sideways along the creaky, snake-thin aisles. This was not a hangout for the Ikea crowd, but for memorabilia lovers, it was Nirvana.

"Mom would love it in here," I said, trying to take everything in. "There's so much stuff I don't know where to start looking."

"Go find someone to help you," Gran suggested. "If there are cookie cutters here, a clerk will know where to find them. I'll just look around while you're gone." Then she turned her attention to a set of flatirons sitting on the shelf of an old pie cupboard.

I had clearly been dismissed, so I slithered past another shopper and headed deeper into the store. In the third room, I found a clerk.

"Cookie cutters?" she said. "Oh, sure. We have all kinds. Follow me."

'All kinds' was right. She took me to a basket that must have contained thirty of them, and they were all different. The prices weren't too bad either, so I rooted out five that looked in pretty good shape — and which I didn't think my mother already owned — and took them to the cashier. Then I went looking for Gran.

At first I couldn't see her and I thought maybe she'd left without me, but after a more thorough search, I discovered her sitting on her haunches in front of a glass display case.

"What have you found?" I asked as I hunkered down beside her.

"Snow globes," she replied, keeping her eyes fixed on the cabinet. "You don't see them around much anymore. Another one of those fads that's had its day. You used to be crazy for them when you were a little girl."

I nodded. "I know. I loved to watch the snow float down and settle on the objects inside. It never landed exactly the same way twice. Of course, I used to hold the globe at odd angles so that the snow would fall in different directions, as if it had been blown by the wind. It made me feel like Mother Nature."

My grandmother laughed and tapped the display window. "Look at that one there — third from the left, middle row. Isn't that like the one I gave you the Christmas before you went to Australia?"

The globe Gran was pointing to was taller than the others and had a perfectly round base. Inside was a tiny church nestled beneath the boughs of a big, bushy evergreen tree.

"It's sort of the same," I said, "but my globe had a log cabin under the fir tree, not a church."

Gran nodded. "That's right. I remember now. Whatever happened to it anyway?"

I shrugged.

Gran sighed and started to push herself up. "Likely as not it got lost in the move."

"Maybe," I mumbled, as I held out a hand to help her.

But my snow globe *hadn't* been lost. In fact, I knew exactly what had happened to it. I'd given it to Charlie.

Charlie had moved into the neighbourhood in January, but by mid-March he still hadn't made any friends. I guess he'd tried, but he wasn't the sort of kid who fit in easily. Maybe it had something to do with his size. Charlie was the same age as everybody else in our class, but he was so big he looked older. That might not have been a huge deal except that he acted way younger, and the combination of those two things made him a misfit. Consequently, nobody tried very hard to get to know him.

He wasn't interested in sports like the other boys, so he couldn't even find a place for himself that way. During recess and lunch hour, he tended to hang out with the girls. He didn't actually do stuff with us; he just kind of hovered in the background, and after a while we stopped noticing he was there.

Anyway, on this particular day I'd taken my snow globe to school. I don't know why. When you're in grade six you just do that sort of thing. The point is that I had it at school, and at recess I took it outside to show my friends. Everybody oohed and ahed appropriately, shook it a few times, and then broke off in groups to play. So I put the globe on the pavement next to the school and headed off to skip.

At the end of recess when I went back, it was gone. Instantly panicking, I spun around, my eyes searching every inch of pavement. The globe was definitely missing. Either it had been stolen, or somebody was playing a joke on me. I planted myself at the school door, eyeballing everyone as they went inside, trying to decide who looked guilty.

Charlie was last in line. When he got to the door, he stopped and held out the snow globe.

I think my jaw hit the pavement. Charlie Castle was the last person I would have suspected of taking it. He was too honest to be a thief and too clueless to play a practical joke.

"I wasn't going to keep it," he mumbled. "I just wanted to look at it." Fear suddenly contorted his features. "I didn't break it though — honest!" And pushing the globe into my hands, he ran inside.

The rest of the morning I couldn't get Charlie and what he had done out of mind. If he'd wanted to see the snow globe, why hadn't he just said so? When lunch hour rolled around, I decided to ask him.

For once he wasn't hanging around, so I had to go looking for him. I found him hunched on the front steps of the school with his chin propped in his hands.

"Waiting for someone?" I asked, plunking myself down.

He inched away and eyed me suspiciously. "Like who?"

I shrugged. "You tell me."

He frowned and gave his head a shake.

"So how come you're sitting by yourself?" I gestured toward the schoolyard full of laughing, screaming kids. "Why aren't you playing?"

His frown turned into a scowl. "As if you care."

I reached into my jacket pocket for the snow globe and held it out to him.

The way he pulled back you would have thought I was handing him the intestines of a dead cat.

"Here." I shook the globe and held it out again. "Go on. Take it. You said you wanted to hold it. Here's your chance."

Charlie looked uncertain, but he took the globe. Over and over, he shook it and watched the blizzard of snow settle on the fir tree and cabin. He was totally mesmerized, oblivious to the fact that I was still sitting there.

I cleared my throat. "You like it?"

He nodded and shook the globe again. "My dad has a cabin just like this one," he said.

I have to admit I was a bit stunned. Not about Charlie's dad having a cabin, but about Charlie having a dad. Because he was a foster kid, I never thought of him as having parents. And even if he did have them, he didn't live with them, so it was like they didn't count anyway. Of course, I didn't tell Charlie that. All I said was, "Oh, yeah? Is it in the woods?"

He beamed and nodded.

"Have you ever been to it?"

His smile sagged at the edges and he shook his head. "No, but my dad's going to take me there sometime. He promised."

I nodded but didn't say anything.

Charlie's expression brightened again. "I have a picture."

"Of the cabin?"

Another nod.

"Can I see it?"

"I don't have it with me. But maybe sometime."

It was my turn to nod. "Sure. Sometime."

We were quiet for a while, and then out of the blue, Charlie said quietly, "It's my birthday."

I sat up straighter. "Today? Really? I didn't know that, Charlie. Happy Birthday."

A timid smile pulled up the corners of his mouth. "Thanks."

"So what presents did you get?"

The smile disappeared and I realized I'd said the wrong thing. Maybe nobody knew it was Charlie's birthday. Maybe he hadn't gotten any presents.

Suddenly I was angry. That was so wrong! A birthday was a person's very own special day. It was more important than Christmas! But I didn't want to embarrass Charlie by making a fuss, and since biting my tongue was too painful, I decided I should just leave.

"Well, I hope you have a very happy birthday, Charlie," I said, standing up and glancing meaningfully toward the playground. "Jilly's waiting for me. I better go."

"Sure," he mumbled and held out the snow globe. "Thanks."

"You're welcome," I said, ignoring his outstretched hand and jamming my own into my pockets. "I'm glad you like your present. If I'd known it was your birthday, I would have wrapped it. See ya." And then I ran off.

Eight

Charlie and I never talked about the snow globe after that. I never mentioned it to anyone else either. It wasn't a secret; it was just too private to share. And then after a while I forgot about it. If Gran hadn't stopped at that display case in the collectibles shop, the memory might have stayed buried forever.

But thanks to that snow globe, Charlie was front and centre in my thoughts again. What had happened to him? Mrs. Gunderson hadn't given me any answers, but on the return trip from Sidney, I thought of someone who might.

"Do you mind if I borrow your car for an hour, Gran?" I said as we hauled our purchases into the house. "I need to run an errand."

"It's all yours," she replied and handed me the keys. "While you're gone I think I'll sink my teeth into that mystery I bought. I bet I can get through at least two sentences before I nod off. I can't believe how tired I am." As if to prove her point, she yawned. Then she shook her finger at me. "And it's all your fault, young lady. You've tuckered me right out. I haven't walked that much in years!"

I laughed and shrugged. "Sorry, Gran. I keep telling you it's that ocean air. It'll get you every time." I gave her a peck on the cheek and headed back to the car. "See you later."

I had no idea if Detective Celia Norris could help me — or even if she would — but I was about to find out.

The parking lot at the police station was packed. There were only two available spaces near the building. One was reserved for the Chief of Police and the other was designated handicapped parking, neither of which I qualified for — regardless of what my brother might say. I must have cruised that lot for ten minutes looking for a space, but in that entire time, not a single car pulled out. I ended up parking at the far end of the next lot and hiking back.

I'd never been to a police station before, and as I pushed through the front door, I started to feel like a criminal. Me — goody-two-shoes Jessica Lawler who'd never had so much as a parking ticket — was feeling like one of Canada's most wanted — and all because of a dream. The memory of every crime I'd every committed flooded my mind. Jilly and I sneaking out at two in the morning to chuck pebbles at Myles Robinson's bedroom window. I think we woke everyone in the house *except* Myles. Then there were the prank telephone calls we made to markets all over the city. *'Do you have Robin Hood in the bag?' 'Yes.' 'Well, let him out — he's suffocating!'* I'd walked against the light a few times too, and also told my share of white lies. My worst crime though was stealing candy from the corner store. I was only six at the time, and the candy turned out to be a dog cookie — *Yuck, it tasted terrible!* — but that didn't change the fact that I had stolen something.

As I was busy thinking all this, two uniformed officers headed straight for me, and I just about leaped out of my shoes. *They knew!*

Then again, maybe not. Without even glancing in my direction, they walked right on past and out the door.

I took a gulp of air to slow my racing heart and made myself move toward what looked like the ticket booth of a movie theatre — though the sign above claimed it was an information desk.

"Excuse me," I said, stooping to talk through the half moon opening in the glass.

The woman on the other side looked up from a pile of papers she'd been studying. "Yes?" she said. "Can I help you?"

"I would like to speak to Detective Norris," I replied through the opening, trying to sound more confident than I felt.

"It's all right. You don't have to bend over, dear," the woman smiled. "I can hear you just fine."

Sheepishly I straightened up.

"As for speaking to Detective Norris, that might be a bit more of a challenge," she continued.

"If she's not here, I could come back another time," I blurted, "tomorrow or the next day?" I knew I sounded anxious, but I couldn't help it. I needed to find out about Charlie.

The woman shook her head. "I'm afraid that won't help. Detective Norris is on maternity leave right now and will be for a year." My disappointment must have shown, because the woman said, "Perhaps someone else could help you."

Could they? I was doubtful. Detective Norris had been the one in charge of Charlie's case. I frowned. "I-I don't know," I stammered. "I wanted to find out about a missing person. It's an old investigation," I added. "Six years."

The woman turned to her computer and placed her hands on the keyboard. "What is the name of the person who went missing?"

"Charlie. I mean Charles Castle. He was twelve."

As I rattled off everything I knew about Charlie, the woman plugged the information into her computer.

"Ah, yes," she said finally. "There it is. You were right. Celia Norris was in charge of the investigation. But I see here that Constable Stephen Barnes worked on the case too, and if I'm not mistaken he *is* in the building. Let me buzz him."

I wasn't sure if I wanted her to do that or not. I'd had my heart set on speaking to Detective Norris. For one thing she was a woman and therefore less intimidating. Even though I knew police officers were the good guys, they still made me nervous — particularly the men. In their uniforms, they seemed larger than life. The fact that they carried guns didn't help. The other reason I wanted to speak to Celia Norris was because Gran had said she was nice, and I trusted my grandmother's judgment. On the other hand, this Constable Barnes might be my only hope of getting the information I needed.

He didn't keep me waiting long. For some reason I was expecting a young, gruff army-type, but the man who strolled around the corner and up to the information desk was middle-aged with silver hair, a slight build, and a face full of happy lines that made him look like he was perpetually smiling. Right away I started to relax.

Constable Barnes led me to a small windowless room, containing nothing but a round table and four chairs. I wondered if this was where interrogations were conducted and scanned the walls for a one-way mirror. But the only decoration was a large framed photograph of the gardens in front of the municipal offices.

When I had recapped what I knew about Charlie's disappearance — leaving out the part about my dream — Constable Barnes said, "That was a long time ago. Why are you looking for information now?"

"I've been away," I replied. "My family moved to Australia right after Charlie disappeared. I didn't even know he'd gone missing until I came to Victoria this week to visit my grandmother."

Constable Barnes seemed puzzled. "But didn't you say you had been in Victoria when he disappeared?"

"Yes," I admitted, "but I was sick. I had meningitis. I don't remember anything about that time."

He scrunched his forehead and his eyebrows knotted together. After a minute or so, his expression cleared. "That's right. It's all coming back to me now. A girl *was* hospitalized the day of the disappearance." He looked up. "That was you?"

I nodded.

"Celia — I mean Detective Norris — went to the hospital to question you, but you were pretty out of it."

"Really?" I said. "I don't remember."

He smiled. "Well, that's the point, isn't it?" Then he became more serious again. "So have you recovered your memory now? Are you able to tell us something that you couldn't before?"

My stomach did a flip. My recurring nightmare, the flashback in the tree, and then the one in the cornfield — would Constable Barnes consider those things information? Maybe, but more than likely he'd just view them as the ravings of a lunatic and show me the door. Either that or he'd arrest me on the spot, since every bit of evidence I had pointed to me.

I shook my head. "No," I said. "I still don't remember that day. Actually, I was hoping you could tell me something that might jog my memory."

He heaved a sigh. "I see. Well, I can tell you the status of the case. That much is public information. But because the investigation is still ongoing — missing person cases remain open until the person is either found or a body is recovered — I'm not at liberty to go into particulars."

This was not good news, since it was 'the particulars' that I needed. "Oh," I said. Even I could hear the disappointment in my voice. "So what *is* the status of the case?"

"Well, as I said, it's still active. Your friend has not been found," he paused, " — one way or the other, and at this point we have no new leads to follow."

"That's it?"

The lines on his face crinkled into a smile. "I'm afraid so. Anything else is privileged information."

"You can't tell me what the people you questioned said?"

He shook his head. "Sorry."

This was getting me nowhere. "Can you at least tell me *who* you've questioned?"

He shook his head again.

This was so frustrating. "Okay," I said. "What about this? What if a potential witness moved away before she — or he — could be questioned? Would the police track her — or him — down?" As an afterthought I added, "Hypothetically speaking, of course."

Constable Barnes' eyes twinkled. "Hypothetically speaking, you say?" Then his face crinkled into a smile. "Yes, we'd track her — *or him* — down. We absolutely would."

Nine

On the other end of the phone Jilly sounded incredulous. "So the police *did* question Amanda?"

"Constable Barnes didn't say that — at least not in so many words. He couldn't, because the investigation is still open. All he said was that it's standard police procedure to track down and question anyone who might know something about a crime, even if that someone is in another city."

"Like I said," Jilly harrumphed smugly, "they questioned her." Then she added, "So this is good news, right?"

Jilly was a wonderful person and my best friend, but sometimes her tunnel vision could be very frustrating. She only saw things the way she wanted to see them. I took a deep breath in order to keep my cool. "Not necessarily. Even if the police did question her — and we don't know for sure that they did — I still have no idea what Amanda told them."

"Well, you sure as heck know what she *didn't* tell them!" Jilly exclaimed so loudly I had to pull the phone away from my ear. "Since you didn't get thrown in the slammer, you know she didn't tell them you killed Charlie. Which means you *didn't*, which is what I have been saying all along. And that means I am way smarter than you give me credit for and you should start listening to me once in a while."

"Don't break your arm patting yourself on the back," I said. "The way I see it, you're jumping to conclusions."

"What're you talking about?" Jilly fumed. "You know darn well the police talked to Amanda. So if you had whacked Charlie with the shovel, they'd know about it. And you'd be under arrest."

"Unless I did it when Amanda wasn't there? That could have happened too. And if she didn't actually see me do it, she couldn't tell the police a thing, which means they're probably waiting around for me to trip up and give myself away."

"Why are you so determined to be a murderer?" Jilly asked.

Even though I'd been living with the idea for months, it was horrible to hear Jilly say it. I winced. "I'm not. Not really. I'm just trying to look at all the possibilities." I sighed. "I just wish I knew what Amanda had said. It might help me remember."

"Or not," Jilly countered.

"Thanks for the vote of confidence."

"I'm just being realistic," she said. "You should be relieved. A few days ago you were scared spitless you were a killer. Now you know you're not."

"But I *don't* know that. Not for sure." As logical as Jilly made everything sound, there were still too many unanswered questions. Where was Charlie? What had happened to him? And if I hadn't killed him, why was I having that dream? The pieces to the puzzle were in my head — somewhere — I was sure of it. All I had to do was find them and put them together. It was so frustrating. "I just can't remember!" I growled.

"Well, if you want my opinion — and you're getting it whether you want it or not — I think that at some point you *will* remember. You just have to give it time. You also need to chill out. You're wound up so tight your memory couldn't push through if it tried."

"You think?"

"Absolutely. So let's do something tonight to help you relax and take your mind off this whole Charlie business."

"Like what?"

"Well, my running club is doing the Beaver/Elk Lake run in about an hour, and after that we're going to meet up at the Macaroni Grill for supper. Why don't you come along? To dinner, that is. Somehow I can't picture you running ten kilometres," she tacked on snidely.

I ignored the wisecrack. "Thanks anyway, Jilly, but these are *your* friends. You go. I'll catch up with you tomorrow."

"Forget that," Jilly swept away my objection. "You're my friend too, and in another week you'll be back in Calgary. Who knows when I'll see you again? Come on. Come to dinner. You'll like these people. They're fun."

Jilly was right. The people in her running club *were* fun and the change of scenery and faces did help me relax. I didn't think of Charlie all evening — well, at least not until it was nearly over.

As people finished their meals, they started to leave. Soon, Jilly, Myles, and I were the only ones left at the table. The waitress came by with the coffee carafe to fill our cups for the third time.

I put my hand over mine. "No more for me, thanks," I smiled. "If I have another drop I'm going to float away. Come to think of it," I said, catching a special look pass between Jilly and Myles, "I think now would be a good time to visit the ladies' room. If you two will excuse me, I'll be right back."

I stayed extra long in the washroom. The evening had been a lot of fun, but now I almost wished I hadn't come. Clearly, Jilly and Myles wanted some time alone, which they weren't going to get with me around.

When I got back to the table, I made a big production of yawning. "I'm sorry, guys," I said, "but I am totally bagged. My grandmother and I walked all over Sidney this morning and then along the beach this afternoon, and I'm really starting to feel it. If you don't mind, I think I'll call it a night and grab a cab."

"You can't do that," they chorused.

I shrugged. "Sorry, but I have to."

"Get serious," Jilly wailed. "It's not even ten o'clock!"

"I know," I grimaced. "I hate being a wet blanket, but I'm really beat."

Jilly pushed back her chair and stood up. "Well, you're not taking a cab," she stated flatly. "That's just plain silly. I'll drive you home."

"Jilly, I don't want — "

Myles cut me off. "Jilly's right," he said, pushing himself away from the table too.

"But you guys are having such a good time; I don't want to wreck it."

Jilly rolled her eyes. "You're not wrecking anything. Don't be such a goof." Then she winked at Myles and her face split into a huge grin. "We'll just drop you off and then drive up Mt. Doug to make out."

For a second Myles' mouth dropped open. "Jilly!" Even in the dim light of the restaurant, I could see he was blushing.

"I'm kidding!" Jilly laughed, punching him in the arm. "I just like getting a rise out of you. Oops! Bad choice of words." She laughed again.

Myles' face got redder than ever and he suddenly developed a great interest in his shoes.

Still chuckling to herself, Jilly headed for the exit with Myles and me following silently behind. Once outside in the parking lot, Jilly took a deep breath of evening air and declared, "All you really need, Jess, is a little walk to work off dinner. If you're sleepy," she shot me a look that clearly said she didn't think I was, "it's because you've been sitting for three hours with a lump of food in your stomach. A bit of exercise would do you good. It would do us all good."

"What are you talking about?" I retorted. "You guys just ran ten kilometres. What's that if it's not exercise?"

"An appetite stimulant," Jilly said. Then she grabbed Myles' hand and mine and started dragging us toward the car. "Come on. It's the perfect evening for a stroll along the breakwater."

Myles pulled back and pointed across the parking lot. "But what about my car?"

Jilly shrugged. "We'll stop for it on the way back."

Jilly parked on Dallas Road facing the ocean. The moon — a huge white disc just a sliver away from being full — hung low in the sky, turning the water into a sea of glittering sequins, and once again I was reminded of my fifth wheel status. If it weren't for me, Jilly and Myles could be taking full advantage of the romantic setting. I considered staying behind while they walked the breakwater — or better yet, letting them stay behind while I walked it, but I knew they'd never go for either suggestion, so I just kept quiet and let myself out of the car.

It doesn't matter how calm the rest of the city is, it's always blustery on the breakwater, and as we picked our way along the path snaking through the chain link gate, gusts of wind snapped at our clothes and whipped our hair into our faces.

The breakwater is actually a massive wall of concrete blocks jutting out into the sea at Ogden Point — calm and quiet on one side, but a fury of waves on the other. At the far end is a lighthouse with a red concrete base that serves as a canvas for every graffiti artist in the city.

The evening was warm, but even so the sea air had a bite to it, and since none of us was wearing long sleeves, we huddled on the leeward side of the lighthouse for a few minutes to warm up before heading back to land.

"Brrrr," Jilly complained, briskly rubbing her arms. "I forgot how cold it can be out here."

I don't know if that was intended to be a hint, but Myles put his arm around Jilly's shoulder anyway. I turned away to hide a smile.

"It might help if you had some meat on your bones," Myles said.

Bones, bones, Bone Tree Hill — that's all it took to send my thoughts whirling back to Charlie. I gazed into the night, but instead of seeing a sky full of stars, I saw myself wielding a shovel and then Charlie with blood-soaked hair, lying at my feet.

"Jess. Jess!" Jilly was shaking my arm.

"Huh? What?" I pushed through the fog inside my head and pasted a phony smile on my face. "Sorry. I guess I was daydreaming."

"From the look of you, I'd say it was more like a nightmare." Myles' forehead was furrowed with concern. "Are you okay?"

"I'm fine. Really," I insisted when he didn't seem convinced. "I was just — "

"Thinking about Charlie again," Jilly finished my sentence with a resigned shake of her head.

"Jilly," I said through gritted teeth in a tone that clearly implored her not to say anything more. Myles was a nice guy, but there was no way I wanted to share my dark dream with him.

"Who's Charlie?" he asked.

"You know," Jilly said. "That Gunderson foster kid who went missing six years ago."

"Oh, yeah," Myles nodded. "I didn't know the guy personally — I think he was a grade younger than me, but I remember there being a big search when he disappeared."

"He was the same age as Jess and me," Jilly said. "Anyway, Jess was with him the evening he disappeared, but she was sick with meningitis and can't remember a thing. She thought that coming back to Victoria might jog her memory."

I felt myself start to breathe again. Jilly hadn't blabbed my secret.

"I gather that hasn't happened," Myles said.

I shook my head. "Not really. There was another girl with Charlie and me that evening, and I thought that if I got her version of what happened it might help me remember, but she's moved away and the police aren't allowed to disclose what she told them." I shrugged. "So now I'm stuck."

"Who was the girl?" Myles asked.

"Her name is Amanda McCreedy. She only lived in Victoria for a couple of years. Her dad was in the navy and got transferred to Ottawa just after Charlie disappeared."

"Did you say McCreedy?"

I nodded.

"Did this girl, this Amanda — did she have a brother?"

I nodded again. "I think so. But he was like five years older. I didn't know him."

"Me neither," said Myles. "But my brother did. He and Bob McCreedy were friends. In fact, they still are. They exchange emails all the time. Phone calls sometimes too. If you want Amanda's number, I'm pretty sure I can get it for you."

Ten

Myles phoned me with the number first thing the next morning.

I stared at the paper in my hand, unconsciously memorizing the digits. Then I looked up at the clock. It would be nearly noon in Ottawa — no need to worry about getting people out of bed.

"Here goes nothing," I muttered under my breath as I grabbed the phone. I punched in the numbers and waited anxiously for someone to pick up. One ring — what was I going to say to Amanda? It had been six years. I couldn't come right out and ask her what she'd told the police. Two rings — but I couldn't very well make small talk either. Even as kids Amanda and I hadn't been very tight, and then when I moved to Australia we'd lost touch completely. She would have to know there was a reason for my call. Three rings — somebody should have answered by now. A feeling somewhere between panic and disappointment fluttered in my stomach. Maybe no one was home. It was a weekday; everyone was probably at work. I should have called closer to dinnertime. The phone rang again. Voice mail was bound to kick in anytime now, and I did not want to leave a message.

I was just getting set to hang up when a breathless voice on the other end panted, "Hello?"

It was a young woman — Amanda, I assumed — but I didn't know for sure, so I said, "Hello. Is this the McCreedy residence?"

The tone of the voice instantly changed. "Look, if you're trying to sell something, forget it. Even if I had the money, I'm not in the mood. I just about broke my neck getting to the phone. And now I'm standing in a towel, dripping water all over the floor. Why can't you people find — "

"I'm not a telemarketer," I said quickly. "I'm not selling anything, and I'm not a charity looking for a donation. My name is Jessica Lawler, and I'm trying to locate Amanda McCreedy."

Silence.

"Are you still there?" I hadn't heard the phone disconnect, but sometimes you couldn't tell.

"Huh? What? Uh, sorry. Yeah, I'm . . . I'm here." She sounded dazed. "Sorry," she said again. "You caught me off guard. Did you say your name was Jessica Lawler? As in Jessica Lawler from Victoria?"

She sounded so surprised, I couldn't help grinning. "Yes," I replied. "That would be me — except I live in Calgary now. Is this Amanda?"

"Yeah."

"Oh, good." I didn't even try to hide my relief. "I didn't think I was ever going to find you!" Then a vision of Amanda shivering in a towel popped into my head. "But maybe this isn't a good time. I may not be selling anything, but I've still interrupted your shower."

"Forget it. I was done anyway, and I've switched the towel for a robe, so it's all good. Sorry about going off on you like that. I just get so tired of telemarketers. We must get ten calls a week and always at the worst possible time."

I laughed. "I know what you mean. But I swear I'm not looking for money."

"Good to know," Amanda sniggered. Then her voice became serious. "So why *are* you calling?"

I swallowed hard. "You don't beat around the bush, do you?"

This time her laugh was like sandpaper. "Well, it's pretty obvious, don't you think? I mean it's not like we exchange weekly emails. If I'd called you out of the blue, wouldn't you wonder why?"

She had a point.

"How'd you even find me?"

"Myles Robinson," I replied. "His brother and yours keep in touch."

"Do they? I have no clue. My brother moved out on his own a couple of years ago, so I barely see him. Not that we ever talked much anyway." In my mind's eye I could see her shrugging. "It doesn't matter. The point is you found me. The question is why."

The ball was in my court. I felt awkward. It's not that I'd expected this conversation with Amanda to be a walk down memory lane, but I had hoped for a bit of a cushion between "Hello" and "What do you want?"

So much for expectations. I took a deep breath and plunged in.

"Amanda, do you remember the last time we were up on Bone Tree Hill — you, me, and Charlie Castle? It was six years ago, the evening he went missing."

"Yeah, sure. Of course I remember."

"Well, I don't."

There was a pause as Amanda digested what I'd said. "What do you mean, you *don't*? How could you forget something like that?"

"I keep asking myself that same question. Unfortunately the only explanation I can come up with is that I had meningitis. I didn't know it when we were on the hill, but when I got home I collapsed, and my parents had to rush me to the hospital. They say I was out of my head with fever for days, and when I finally came around, I'd lost a whole chunk of my life. I didn't even know that Charlie had disappeared until I came back to Victoria this week to visit my grandmother."

"Are you serious?" I could almost see Amanda's mouth hanging open. "You don't remember *anything* about that day? Nothing at all?"

"I'm not sure," I said hesitantly. I didn't know how much I should tell Amanda. The line between what I remembered and what I had dreamed was pretty hazy. "I think I remember you and me lying on our backs in the gully below Bone Tree Hill, looking up at the clouds. Did we do that?"

"Yeah."

"And then Charlie came along, and we hid behind a bush so he wouldn't see us. Did we do that too?"

"Uh-huh. And then I sneezed, and Charlie started chasing us. Do you remember that?"

"Yes," I said, "I do. But after that everything goes blank." That wasn't completely true, but I couldn't bring myself to tell Amanda what I'd seen in my dream.

"Holy shit!" she exclaimed. "How could you forget *that*? It's the best part!" She was clearly warming up to the subject. "Charlie was madder than I had ever seen him. He was out for blood, and he chased us for ages — well, actually, he chased *me* — you might as well not even have been there. Not that I'm surprised, mind you. Charlie would never have laid a finger on you no matter how crazy he got."

I pulled back and stared at the phone for a second. What was that supposed to mean? I would have asked, but Amanda was barrelling on with her story and I didn't want to miss a single detail.

"Anyway, I was getting so tired, I could barely lift my feet, so — wouldn't you know it — I stumbled over a rock and fell on my face. That was all the opportunity Charlie needed. He had a shovel in his hand, and he threw it at my head. It just missed! You gotta know that got me moving again. Tired or not, I jumped up as fast as I could, but before I could put any distance between us, Charlie grabbed my shoulders and began shaking the hell out of me. He shook me so hard my brain rattled. I'm not kidding! My brain was bouncing around inside my head like a ping-pong ball. I couldn't even see straight. Everything was a blur. I seriously thought he was going to kill me."

"So what happened next?" I said, though I was pretty sure I knew.

"Suddenly you showed up out of nowhere. You were waving the shovel at Charlie and screaming at him to let me go."

I could feel every muscle in my body tensing up. This was it. "And did he?" I could barely get the question past the tightness in my throat.

"At first I don't think he heard you — he was concentrating too hard on shaking the stuffing out of me, but then you moved into his line of vision and told him that if he didn't stop you were going to clobber him with the shovel."

I gasped. I couldn't help it. I had dreamed that scene so many times, but hearing the words come out of Amanda's mouth shocked me all over again.

"Did I?" I asked fearfully. "Hit him, I mean?"

To my surprise, Amanda laughed. "Yeah, right. Like that would ever happen. You would never even smack a mosquito. So do you actually think you would've hit Charlie? Get real."

"So I *didn't* hit Charlie with the shovel?" I was still holding my breath.

"You sure looked like you were going to — I'll give you that," Amanda chuckled. "You had that shovel cocked back like a baseball bat, and you looked ready to let 'er rip. I guess Charlie thought so too, because as soon as he saw you he stopped. Just like that."

"So I didn't hit him?" I said again.

"Isn't that what I just said? Are you hard of hearing or what?" she snapped. "No, you didn't hit him."

I was beginning to remember why I had never liked Amanda much.

"So what happened next?" I asked.

"Well, for a good minute Charlie didn't do anything except stare at you. He was still hanging on to my shoulders, but he wasn't shaking me anymore. He was just staring like he'd never seen you before."

"But why?" I hadn't meant to say that out loud.

"Are you kidding!" Amanda guffawed. "That big goon had it for you so bad, you could practically see him drooling whenever you were around. And there you were, threatening to knock his block off. You couldn't have hurt him more if you *had* smacked him with that shovel."

My heart clenched.

"So what did he do?" My voice was barely a whisper.

"He started to cry. Can you believe it? A great big guy like that, and he starts blubbering like a baby. Anyhow, he let go of me — that's all I cared about. Then he grabbed the shovel from you and started running for the Gunderson farm, bawling all the way. So I ran too — in the opposite direction, of course. I never stopped or even slowed down until I got home. I didn't even look back, so I have no idea what you did after I took off."

Unfortunately neither did I.

I had been so sure the memory of that day would come back to me once I heard what Amanda had to say. But it hadn't, and I couldn't have been more deflated if I'd been run over by a steamroller.

Amanda and I talked for another five minutes, catching up on the last six years. Not that it mattered. The evening on Bone Tree Hill was the only thing that connected us, and though it had left a scar, it hadn't brought us close. In fact, our lives would probably never intersect again, and that was just fine with me.

Eleven

After I got off the phone, I sat for a while and thought about what Amanda had said. I'd threatened Charlie with the shovel, but I hadn't hit him with it. I tried to convince myself that meant I was innocent. I hadn't killed Charlie. But deep inside, I knew that wasn't true. Amanda might not have seen anything, but that didn't mean it didn't happen. I could have hit Charlie after she left. The vision of him lying in his own blood flashed in my brain, and I shuddered. The image was so vivid, so real. Charlie was dead, and more and more it felt like I was the one who had killed him.

But I had to know for sure. If it turned out to be true, I had no idea what I would do, but I still had to know.

I went hunting for Gran. I found her lounging on the deck, totally immersed in her mystery novel. She looked so content I hated to disturb her, so I jotted a note to let her know where I was going and set off for Bone Tree Hill.

The morning was warm enough, but the sun was playing hide 'n' seek with the clouds, and with every mood swing the day took, I found myself getting more and more agitated. A tiny daisy waved gaily from its unlikely home in the middle of the path, and I ground it under my heel with only the smallest twinge of guilt.

Everything was still a mystery. I hadn't gotten my memory back, I had no idea what had happened to Charlie, and half of my dream was still unexplained. There were those flashbacks in the tree and the cornfield too. I had no clue what they meant either.

Why couldn't I remember?

It made me want to scream. The memories were there. I could feel them. They were like butterfly kisses tickling the edges of my mind — maddeningly close but impossible to catch. I could almost see them too — gauzy ghosts from the past, floating into my brain for a split second and then vanishing before I could get a good look at them. Hopefully Jilly was right, and it was just a matter of time before everything came clear. Otherwise I was going to go mad.

I couldn't stop thinking about Charlie. *Had* he run away? With all my heart, I hoped that was what had happened. Amanda said he'd felt betrayed when I threatened him with the shovel. She said he'd cried and run off. In my mind I saw him running to the Gunderson farm, but what if that wasn't where he'd gone? What if everything had finally become too much for him and he'd run away for real? There was no telling where he might have gone. If he'd hitched a ride, he could have ended up at the other end of the island. If a pervert had picked him up, he — I shuddered — I didn't want to think about that. Then again, maybe Charlie had gone looking for his dad's cabin. He hadn't said where it was — he probably didn't even know, but if he'd headed into the wilderness, it wouldn't have taken him long to get lost. And then what? He probably didn't have any survival skills. No weapons either — unless he'd taken the shovel with him. There were bears and cougars in the woods. I shuddered again. I didn't want to think about that either.

It didn't matter how many scenarios I imagined, I knew that none of them had happened. Charlie hadn't run away. He had died. That was the only explanation for the bloody vision in my dream.

Round and round in my brain, my thoughts chased one another, like a relentless game of tag, until my head felt like it was going to explode. *Tag* — you killed Charlie. *Tag* — but I couldn't have. *Tag* —

"Stop it!" I scolded myself aloud. "Stop it, stop it, stop it!" I went to boot a stone but missed and stirred up a cloud of dust instead, which I then proceeded to choke on. Jilly was right. I was obsessed with that stupid dream. Why couldn't I let it go? Why was I determined to turn it into something it wasn't? Hadn't Amanda already shot holes in it? I hadn't killed Charlie; I'd only made him cry, and people didn't die from crying. It was time for me to wake up. The dream wasn't a memory. It wasn't an omen. It was a dream. That's all.

I continued up the trail. But my resolve was short-lived, and by the time I reached the top I was as determined as ever to get my memory back and solve the mystery of Charlie's disappearance.

Maybe it would help if I recreated the scene. With that thought in mind, I started to wander through the gully. Where had Charlie been when he was shaking Amanda? And where had I been standing with the shovel? I tried to find exactly the same spot. It took a while, but eventually everything looked like it had in my dream — except that the only person acting out a part was me.

I took my place, imagining Charlie and Amanda in front of me. I waited for a memory to kick in, but nothing happened. I raised my arms as if I was wielding the shovel. It didn't make any difference. It was still just the gully and me. Then I had another thought. Amanda said I'd moved around so that Charlie could see me. I altered my position accordingly, but that didn't help either.

I heaved a frustrated sigh and let my arms drop to my sides. This was hopeless.

Discouraged, I trudged up the remaining incline to the top of the hill and did a slow three–hundred-and-sixty-degree pivot. The surrounding countryside was lush and serene — the sort of scenery that inspired poetry. God's country — that's what Gran called it. If this was what Heaven was like, it would suit me fine. Then again, maybe it wasn't Heaven at all. Maybe it was just a wicked trick of the Devil — a phoney cover to dupe the gullible. No one would ever suspect that something horrible had happened here. And yet it had. I was sure of it.

I spun around and slammed my hands against the oak tree. Its rough grey bark bit into my palms. "Tell me what you know!" I shouted. "Show me what you saw!" I leaned into the tree, willing it to acknowledge me, and then I threw my head back and stared up into its branches. From where I was standing they seemed to stretch across the entire valley and right up into the sky.

Then the strangest thing happened. Though my feet never left the ground, I felt myself suddenly shooting up through the tree — like a bullet — whizzing past leaves and branches so fast they became a blur. The ride went on forever and yet it was over before I could blink, and when I caught my breath, I was on top of the world. Actually, I was on top of the oak tree, but I might as well have been on top of the world. I could see everything.

I could see —

I gasped and reeled away from the tree, peering toward the Gunderson farm and the jumble of bushes at the bottom of the hill.

He wasn't there, but I could see him. "Charlie?" I breathed. "Charlie." Then I started forward, slowly at first — as if he would disappear if I moved too quickly. I shut my eyes, but he was still there in the darkness behind my eyelids. I wasn't imagining him; I was remembering.

Having assured myself of that, I flew down the hill almost faster than my legs could carry me and skidded to a stop within inches of the hedge. I stared hard at the grass at my feet and — as clearly as if Charlie was actually there — I saw the shovel on the ground beside his body, its blade red with blood. This was where Charlie had died. Right here on this spot. Not in the gully. I'd been wrong about that; I'd misread the dream. The gully is where I'd threatened Charlie with the shovel, but this was where he'd died.

As the realization sank in, I started to shake. Charlie was really dead. I'd known all along his death was a possibility, but I'd held onto the hope that my dream was wrong. My knees buckled and I sank to the ground. I didn't even try to break my fall. I just crumpled onto the grass like a rag doll and buried my face in my arms, letting a tidal wave of grief wash over me.

"Oh, Charlie," I cried. "Oh, Charlie. I am so sorry."

My heart ached for the boy I had barely known. The boy I had teased. The boy I had ignored. The boy I had killed. But *why* would I kill Charlie? It didn't make any sense. I wasn't a violent person. It had to have been an accident. Unless I'd simply snapped. I'd been so sick. My body had been on fire and my head had been ready to explode. Maybe I'd lost control and lashed out.

I don't know how long I lay on the grass, mourning Charlie and beating myself up for his death, but after a time, I forced myself to sit up and look around. And that's when it hit me. What had started out as a scary dream had turned into a real-life crime. Charlie wasn't a missing person; he was a murder victim. And from the way the evidence was mounting up, I was his murderer.

My heart skipped a beat, and I nervously glanced around. It had been six years — the police weren't likely to be lurking in the bushes, waiting for me to return to the scene of the crime — but I still felt uneasy. This was where Charlie had died — where I had killed him. Where *somebody* had killed him, I corrected myself angrily. Maybe it *wasn't* me. Maybe someone else was responsible for Charlie's death. With all my heart I wanted that to be true, but it was getting harder to believe it. *If only I could remember!*

Little by little, bits and pieces of that evening had started coming back to me, though my brain seemed reluctant to give me the whole story. It was frugally doling out memories one at a time. That didn't mean I couldn't do some real life digging while I waited for the next memory to arrive.

I was so exhausted and frustrated from trying to make sense of my nightmare that for a second I considered telling the police everything I knew — or had dreamed — and let them figure it out, even if it meant being exposed as a killer. I dismissed the thought almost before I finished thinking it. For one thing, the prospect of going to jail was terrifying, but even if I confessed to killing Charlie, the police were going to want details. They were also going to want a body or — at the very least — a murder weapon. And at the moment I couldn't give them any of those things. All I had to offer was a scary dream and a few memory scraps. I needed more.

I started poking around the grass below the bushes. I had no idea what I was looking for, and even if I had, it was unlikely that anything would still be there after all this time. Perhaps this was where I had buried Charlie. I shook my head. Impossible. Freshly dug ground is hard to miss; the police would have seen it right away, which meant I must have disposed of the body some other way. The question was *where?* And, more importantly, *how?* Charlie was a big kid. Jilly was right — it would have been practically impossible for me to move the body by myself. So maybe I'd had help. But *who?* There had to be a clue somewhere.

I moved around to the other side of the hedge, but the fence stopped me from going any farther. I climbed onto the lowest wire rung, stared at the Gunderson farm, and allowed my thoughts to wander.

I tried to remember everything I could about Charlie, but the truth was that I really didn't know very much. I'd never bothered to find out. I'd been too busy being a kid. I hadn't given much thought to the little bit I did know. I was ashamed to admit it — even to myself — but I hadn't ever really paid attention to Charlie. He had just been there, like the grass and the tree and the hill.

I scoured my mind for something — *anything* that would tell me about Charlie. Mostly, there were just remnants of memories — Charlie bellowing and chasing Amanda, Jilly, and me or just looking confused and standing off on his own. I tried to picture him laughing, but all I could come up with was his timid, crooked smile one summer day.

Amanda was in Vancouver visiting relatives, and Jilly had a dental appointment, so I was on my own. After passing a boring morning at home, I decided to pack a picnic lunch and head up to Bone Tree Hill.

It was a really warm day, and when I got to the top, I was sweating. I could feel the heat radiating from my body — it was like I was one big pulse. I gulped down some water, splashed some more on my face, and flopped onto the ground. Then I shut my eyes and leaned against the tree.

It felt wonderful sitting there, knowing the world was just on the other side of my eyelids — the rolling fields, the blue sky, the sunshine — all right there. Birds were soaring above me and chirping up a storm, and a feathery breeze was sliding softly over my skin. It was all good.

And then something bopped me on the head. I opened my eyes in time to see an acorn bounce off a rock beside me and roll away. I clucked my tongue and shut my eyes again. Not thirty seconds later, I got bopped again.

"What the — " I muttered, shielding my eyes and frowning up into the tree.

An acorn smacked me right between the eyes. It didn't hurt, but I jumped to my feet and peered skyward. There was a rustling of leaves, and then a big head with unruly black hair peeked through them.

"Charlie Castle!" I exclaimed. "What's the big idea?"

I tried to sound gruff even though I wasn't really mad, but I guess Charlie could tell, because he smiled that shy smile of his and shrugged. "It was a joke. Pretty funny, eh?"

"Ha, ha," I said, picking up an acorn and chucking it back at him. "What are you doing up there anyway?"

"Waiting."

"For what?"

"For you. And Jilly and Amanda."

"Why? We never said we'd be here today."

He started to climb down the tree. "You're always here."

"Not always," I countered. I didn't like the idea of being predicable.

"Mostly always," Charlie said. "So I was waiting." Then he added, "And practicing."

"Practicing what?" I asked, as I pulled a small blanket from my backpack and spread it onto the grass.

"Practicing being a forest ranger. That's what I'm going to be when I grow up."

"Oh, yeah?" I replied absently, laying my lunch on the blanket.

"Yeah. I saw a program about forest rangers on television. They sit up in a tower, watching for poachers and forest fires. It's an important job and I want to do it."

I nodded, not that I knew anything about forest rangers, but Charlie seemed to, so that was good enough for me. At the moment I was more interested in having lunch.

I glanced at my watch. "Well, it looks like it's lunchtime," I announced. "I guess you should be getting back to the farm. Mrs. Gunderson is probably waiting for you."

The sparkle that had lit up Charlie's eyes when he'd been talking about forest rangers disappeared, and he shook his head.

"Do you make your own lunch?" I asked.

He shrugged, lowered his eyes, and scuffed the ground with his shoe. "Sometimes," he said quietly.

"What about today?"

He gave his head a quick shake, but didn't look up.

"You have to eat, Charlie!" I said, grabbing his wrist and dragging him toward the blanket. "Come on. You can have lunch with me. I made a picnic. It'll be fun."

Charlie looked up. "Really?" he said.

I rolled my eyes. "It's not a big deal. There's lots of food, and like I said, you gotta eat."

"Yeah, that's right" he nodded as he plunked himself down on the blanket and helped himself to a sandwich, a sparkle once more lighting up his eyes. "I gotta eat. Thanks, Jessica."

Twelve

Perhaps Nils Gunderson had been there all along and I had been too preoccupied to notice, or maybe he'd sneaked up on me. I have no clue. All I know is that I was totally caught off guard when he grabbed me by the shoulder and hauled me off the fence.

"What are you — " With flailing arms, I stumbled backwards into the hedge of honeysuckle and wild roses. Branches rustled and snapped as I sank into them, but then sprang back up, bouncing me onto my feet again. It was the same sensation as falling onto a trampoline — only pricklier.

I rubbed my scratched arms and glared at the man standing in front of me, too mad to realize he was glaring at me too. "What did you do that for?"

"You are trespassing," he growled. He spoke with an accent and his voice was much deeper than I remembered. It could have belonged to a man twice his size. It took me by surprise, but I didn't back down.

I jabbed a finger toward the ground. "This is not your property. It belongs to the Stevensons, and they don't care if people are on it. Besides, if I'm trespassing, so are you."

His eyes narrowed dangerously and — if possible — his expression became even fiercer. He grabbed the wire fence and shook it. "This fence *is* my property, and you were climbing it."

Considering he'd just dragged me off, there didn't seem much point denying the fact, so I shrugged with feigned indifference. "So what?"

To my shock and horror, his hand snaked out and clamped onto my arm. I tried to squirm free, but that only made him tighten his grip.

"Ow!" I winced. "You're hurting me." I tried to pry his fingers loose, but he grabbed that hand too. Mr. Gunderson might have been small, but he was strong. I wriggled and tugged, but it didn't do any good. I was trapped — and beginning to panic. He was standing so close I could smell his sweat and feel the heat from his skin. I opened my mouth to scream.

He actually started to laugh. "Go ahead," he sneered. "No one will hear you."

He was right. Aside from the Gunderson farm, there wasn't another house for half a mile. The scream dried up in my throat.

"Why are you doing this?" I whimpered, my earlier bravado gone. "What do you want from me?"

He shoved his face close to mine. His eyes were as grey as storm clouds and every bit as threatening. His teeth were yellow, and his breath smelled of cigarettes. He gave my arm another vicious shake. I flinched.

"I know who you are. Don't think I've forgotten," he snarled. His stare was piercing. I tried to look away, but I couldn't. "I also know you've been poking around and asking questions. The past is the past. If you knew what was good for you, you'd leave it there." His fingers dug deeper into my arm, and he twisted it until it felt like it was going to pop out of the socket. I gasped. His lips peeled back into a malicious grin. "Does that hurt? It would be a good thing to remember." His expression turned stony again and through clenched teeth he growled, "Stay away from my farm."

Then he released his hold on me and strode away. Just like that. I would have run, but my knees gave out and once again I found myself in the hedge. Tears sprang to my eyes, but they had nothing to do with the twigs and thorns clawing at me. In fact I barely felt them as I watched the retreating figure of Nils Gunderson turn into a blur.

When he had disappeared from view, I dragged myself out of the hedge and climbed the hill. My legs felt like rubber, but a horrible fear that Mr. Gunderson would return made me push on. The second I reached the top, I collapsed in a heap beneath the tree and stared numbly back the way I'd come, reliving what had just happened.

I was a wreck. I couldn't stop trembling, and I couldn't think straight. All I wanted was to get far away from the Gunderson farm — as fast as I could. Run to Gran. Tell her what had happened — how Nils Gunderson had threatened me. He might not have come right out and said he was going to kill me, but that's what he meant. He'd told me to leave the past alone. And then he'd twisted my arm until I was sure it was going to break.

But why threaten me? I was just trying to get my memory back. Why would Mr. Gunderson care about that, unless . . .

I stared hard at the hedge again to reassure myself he was really gone.

Had Nils Gunderson killed Charlie? Is that why he didn't want me stirring up the past? Was he afraid I was going to discover the truth about what he'd done? Or . . .

"*I know who you are,*" he'd said. "*Don't think I've forgotten.*"

A lump the size of a baseball lodged itself in my throat, and I started to shake all over again.

Maybe he knew *I'd* killed Charlie. Maybe he'd seen me do it.

I'm not sure how long I sat on Bone Tree Hill, but it was well past lunchtime before I got back to my grandmother's house. It took me that long to pull myself together. Despite the almost overwhelming need to tell Gran and the police how Mr. Gunderson had attacked me, I knew that would be a mistake. For one thing, I'd be making accusations without any proof, so even if the police believed me, there wasn't anything they could do. More importantly, if I opened my mouth, Mr. Gunderson might make good on his threat. So I did the only thing I could think of — the thing I always did when I was stuck — I went to Jilly.

"All that stuff happened *today?*" Jilly's eyes were practically bugging out of her head. "You talked to Amanda, you remembered where Charlie was killed, *and* you had a run-in with Mr. Gunderson?"

"It was a bit more than a run-in," I glowered. "The man threatened to kill me and practically tore my arm out of its socket!"

"So you think he's the one who murdered Charlie?"

I shook my head. "I don't know."

She made a face. "What's not to know? The guy is meaner than a sack of killer bees."

I rubbed my sore arm. "Tell me about it." I felt my forehead bunch together. "But *why* would he kill Charlie? What motive would he have?"

"What motive would anyone have? Charlie was a bit — "
Jilly paused, as if she was searching for the right word,
" — different."

"Okay, so he didn't fit in very well. I admit that. But I don't
think anybody hated him. I didn't. Did you?"

Jilly took her time thinking about that. Finally she shook
her head. "No, I guess I didn't hate him. He frustrated the hell
out of me sometimes — most of the time, actually — but I
didn't hate him. But that doesn't change the fact that he's dead.
Somebody must've had a reason for killing him."

"Maybe not," I mumbled, knowing that if I had murdered
Charlie, I certainly hadn't meant to.

"What do you mean?"

"Maybe the murder wasn't premeditated."

"You think it was an accident?"

I shrugged. "Maybe — or maybe it just wasn't planned."

Jilly looked confused.

"You know," I said, "one of those heat-of-the-moment
things."

She didn't seem convinced. If she knew I still thought I was
the main suspect, she'd have a cow. So I used Mr. Gunderson
as my hypothetical example instead.

"Think about it," I said. "If Mr. Gunderson had planned
to kill Charlie, why would he have used a shovel? Why not
run him over with a tractor or drop him in the middle of the
ocean — make it look like an accident? And why would he have
done it out in the open. If he'd meant to kill Charlie he would
have picked someplace more private, and he would have used a
different weapon. The only reason he used a shovel is because
it was handy."

"So you think this was a crime of passion?"

I nodded. "Sure. Why not. Maybe Charlie made Mr. Gunderson so mad that he smacked him with the shovel."

"And you saw him do it."

"*No!* I mean, I don't know."

"Well, why else would he have threatened you? I think he knows you saw him kill Charlie, so he scared the bee-jeebies out of you to make sure you don't tell anybody."

"But I don't remember anything!" I wailed.

"*He* doesn't know that. He probably thinks you're getting set to spill the beans."

"Do you think he'd actually follow through with his threat?"

"You mean kill you?"

I shuddered. "Do you have to put it that way?"

"What other way is there?"

I pushed the thought out of my mind. "So now what am I supposed to do?"

Jilly shrugged. "I guess that's up to you. In another week you'll be heading back to Calgary. All you have to do between now and then is steer clear of Bone Tree Hill, hope you don't have any more close encounters with Mr. Gunderson, and life will go on as usual for everyone."

"Yeah, everyone except Charlie."

"I never said it was the perfect solution," Jilly pointed out.

"There has to be another option."

"Well, you could always go to the police with what you know."

"And get thrown in jail."

Jilly pulled back. "What are you talking about?"

I clucked my tongue and scowled. "Don't you get it? There is way more evidence pointing to me as the murderer than to Mr. Gunderson."

Jilly put her finger to her head like the muzzle of a gun and pulled the imaginary trigger. "Oh, please. That has got to be the dumbest thing you have ever said. This little nightmare fetish of yours is getting way out of control, Jess. I mean it. You're basing everything on that stupid dream." I opened my mouth to argue, but she cut me off. "I don't care how real it seems to you, that dream is not — I repeat — *not* evidence. Except maybe to prove you're crazy. But don't worry. If they throw you in the loony bin, I promise I'll come visit."

Thirteen

I had the dream again that night. But this time it didn't frighten me. I had accepted that Charlie was dead, and despite Jilly's protests to the contrary, I was fairly certain that I was the one who had killed him. Not that I was comfortable with the idea. What decent person would be? In fact, any time I really thought about it, I fell completely to pieces, crying and shaking uncontrollably. The only straw I had to cling to was knowing I wasn't a murderer at heart. As both Jilly and Amanda had pointed out, I wasn't normally violent. If I had killed Charlie, there had to be extenuating circumstances. But what? What could possibly have made me commit such a brutal act?

Hoping the dream would provide the answers I needed, I studied it carefully, searching for even the slightest clue. How I could do that while I was deep asleep I have no idea, but I did. It was like there were two of me — the one who was dreaming and the one who was trying to make sense of it all.

The next morning I was up with the sun. I even beat Gran out of bed, which was probably a good thing, since it saved me from having to explain where I was going at the crack of dawn. Tiptoeing around the kitchen, I grabbed a muffin and banana and scribbled a quick note.

Dear Gran,

I'm wide awake at six o'clock, so I've gone for a walk. I'll be back in a couple of hours. If Jilly calls, tell her I'm hunting for treasure.

Love Jessica

Then I let myself out the back door and padded across the dewy grass to the garden shed. As I opened the door, sunlight streamed inside, sending all the night critters into hiding. Shovels hung in a tidy row on the back wall. I looked them over and then grabbed the smallest one. It was a long climb up Bone Tree Hill, and there was no sense lugging around more weight than I needed.

I was surprised at how good I felt. After yesterday's clash with Mr. Gunderson, I had been temporarily derailed. The man had really shaken me up. Yet here I was — the very next day — heading back to Bone Tree Hill. It was amazing how a few hours of think time and a good night's sleep could change my perspective. Threats or not, I had to try to get to the bottom of Charlie's death. I wouldn't be able to live with myself otherwise. I just wanted to remember what I already knew, and after last night's dream I had an idea how to achieve that.

Whenever I'd had the dream in the past, I'd been so unnerved by the horror of it, I hadn't been able to focus on anything but Charlie's death. Last night though, I saw the dream in a totally different light, and for the first time, I paid attention to the box Charlie had buried. He was obviously trying to hide it. Was that why I had killed him? Was that what he had died for?

When I reached the top of Bone Tree Hill, I looked long and hard toward the hedge. There was no way I wanted to get ambushed again, especially while I was digging up incriminating evidence.

In my mind I tried to picture Charlie burying the box. His back was to the gully, which meant he'd been on the side of the tree farthest from the Gunderson farm. Perhaps he suspected someone might come after him and he was trying to keep from being seen. That would certainly account for the way he'd exploded when he realized Amanda and I had been watching him.

I walked around the tree a few times, trying to decide where to dig. There were large boulders circling the base of the trunk — exposed roots too, but it was a big tree, and that still left a lot of open ground. So I finally just picked a spot and leaned on the shovel.

An hour later my clothes were drenched with perspiration, there were blisters on my hands, my back felt like it was going to snap in two, and I had turned up enough soil to start a small garden, but I still hadn't found the box. It wasn't there. That could mean only one thing. Someone had gotten to it before me. Tossing the shovel aside, I glanced uneasily toward the Gunderson farm. I couldn't see anyone, but I had an uncomfortable feeling I was being watched.

"You are so predictable," a voice said, and I literally jumped.

In one motion, I spun around and snatched up the shovel.

"Whoa, whoa, whoa!" Jilly hollered as she hopped backwards and raised her hands to protect herself.

"Jilly Carlisle!" I roared, throwing the shovel down again. "I could wring your neck. What the heck are you doing sneaking up on a person like that? You scared the hell out of me!"

"Sorry," she grimaced apologetically. "I wasn't *trying* to scare you. I could have been jingling like Santa's sleigh, and I still don't think you would've heard me. You were in your own little world."

I picked up a clump of dirt and chucked it at her. She deflected it with her back.

"Well, you still scared me," I groused.

"Hey, I said I was sorry." She shook the crumbs of dirt from her clothes and hair. "Thanks a lot." Then she sized up my morning's handy work. "So what's the treasure you're hunting for?"

"You talked with Gran?"

She nodded. "So why are you digging up the tree?"

"I'm not," I snapped, still irked at being ambushed. "I'm trying to find the box Charlie buried. You know — the one in my dream."

"Why?"

"Because I thought maybe that was the reason I — he was killed. I thought there might have been something important in the box."

"Like what?"

"I don't know!" I exploded. "Money maybe. A key. A map. A piece of jewellery. The deed to the ranch. How do I know?"

Jilly raised her hands defensively. "You don't have to bite my head off. I was just asking."

"Well, it doesn't matter anyway," I continued, only slightly less hostile, "because the box isn't here. Somebody else must've already dug it up."

"Yeah, like the police," Jilly said.

"Why do you say that?"

"Because Amanda would've told them about Charlie burying something. And you gotta know they would've checked it out. Right?"

I nodded grudgingly. I had been thinking Mr. Gunderson was the one who had retrieved the box. If it contained incriminating evidence, he would know that I was Charlie's killer, and that would explain why he had attacked me. But if the police had dug it up, then the box wasn't important after all. It was just another dead end.

I slumped against the tree and heaved a frustrated sigh. "I'm right back where I started — half a memory and no proof. No body, no weapon, no evidence. In five days I go back to Calgary and my dream still won't be resolved."

"Okay," said Jilly, "supposing you don't remember everything before you go back to Calgary. That doesn't mean you won't *ever* remember. Like I told you before, it's just a matter of time. Don't sweat it. If you don't get Charlie's killer today, you'll get him next month or next year. There's no statute of limitations on murder, you know."

I shook my head in disbelief. Jilly never ceased to amaze me. "No, I didn't know," I replied. "So how come you do?"

She shrugged. "I saw it on some lawyer show. The point is Charlie's killer is going to get caught sooner or later."

Considering that was me, it wasn't a very comforting thought. I wanted to know the truth, but at the same time, I didn't.

"I have an idea," Jilly said.

"What?" I was all out of ideas myself.

"It seems to me that maybe you need to change your approach," she said.

"Like how?"

"Well, instead of working so hard to *remember* what happened that day, why not look at the clues you've already dug up," she glanced toward the clumps of newly turned earth beneath the tree and grinned, "and try to *figure out* what happened?"

I ignored Jilly's play on words and pointed toward the hedge. "You mean like the fact that Charlie was killed over there?" Then I added, "With the shovel."

Jilly nodded. "Exactly. What else do you know?"

I thought for another minute. "I know Charlie buried a box, but I don't know what was in it, and — if you're right and the police have it — then it probably isn't a clue."

"Don't jump to conclusions," Jilly cautioned me. "You may not know how the box is connected, but it's still a clue. What else?"

"Well, I know Mr. Gunderson threatened me," I said.

"Right," Jilly nodded enthusiastically. "And that goes to motive."

I made a face. *And that goes to motive?* What are you — a closet lawyer?"

"Well, it does!" Jilly protested. "People don't go around threatening other people for no reason."

"Fine," I conceded. "So now we've established what I know — which isn't much, and unless you can read more into it than I do, Miss Sherlock Holmes, I don't think we're any farther ahead."

Jilly didn't even acknowledge my sarcasm. Instead she looked toward the hedge. "The body was over there, right?"

"Right."

"So where did it go?"

"If I knew that, we wouldn't be standing here playing twenty questions," I retorted irritably. "If you have an idea, Jilly, just spit it out!"

"The police didn't find a body. So where did it go?" she persisted. Then sensing I was about to erupt again, she quickly rephrased her question. "Where *could* it have gone?"

I forced myself to calm down and think. "Considering that after Charlie went missing, Mr. Gunderson built a fence with Keep Out signs everywhere and he threatened to hurt me if I didn't stay away from his farm, the body is probably stashed there."

Jilly bobbed her head. "That's what I'm thinking too. It's looking more and more like Mr. Gunderson is our murderer, don't you think?"

When I didn't answer, Jilly glared hard at me and carried on. "Trust me — it does and he is. And it stands to reason that wherever he put the body, he put the shovel too. I mean, he wouldn't want to stick it back in the tool shed, now would he? The police would find it for sure." She paused. "But it's a huge farm. Where would be a good place to lose a body and a shovel? And how would Mr. Gunderson have moved the body? Charlie was a big boy, and Mr. Gunderson is not a big man."

I gingerly touched my arm. It was still sore. "But he is strong."

And then a thought struck me. Maybe Mr. Gunderson *did* move the body. I killed Charlie, and he hid him. I had no idea why he would do that, but like the other pieces of this nightmare puzzle, I had a feeling it would eventually fall into place.

"Fair enough," Jilly shrugged, "but he still had to cross that open field. I don't care how strong he is, that's a huge dead weight to carry or drag any distance."

I clucked my tongue and made a face. "Would you knock off with the puns already?"

Jilly frowned. "What puns?"

"Dead weight?"

She grinned. "Oops. Sorry. I didn't do that one on purpose. But you gotta admit it was pretty good."

I rolled my eyes.

"Anyway," she jumped back on topic, "how did he move the body? Wheel barrow ya think?"

I shook my head. "No. Tractor."

"Really?" Jilly said. "How about his truck?"

I shook my head again. "No. It was the tractor. Mr. Gunderson had been bailing hay that day, and the tractor was still in the field. He wrapped Charlie and the shovel in a tarp, loaded them onto the tractor and drove back to the farm."

Jilly seemed to consider my words before answering. "That's a pretty good theory."

I had been staring at the Gunderson farm as I spoke, but now I turned to look at Jilly. "It isn't a theory," I told her bluntly. "That's what happened. I saw it."

Jilly's eyes suddenly became enormous. "You *did*? You mean you remember?"

I blinked stupidly at Jilly. I was just as stunned as she was. The reality of the situation began to sink in. Finally I nodded and croaked, "Yes."

She swallowed hard, as if her next words were stuck in her throat. When she did get them out, they arrived in a whisper. "Do you remember where Mr. Gunderson took Charlie?"

I didn't answer right away. I needed a minute to get used to this new memory before I shared it.

Jilly waited patiently.

"Yes," I replied finally. "I do."

Fourteen

A s I recounted the memory to Jilly, I felt as though I was in a trance.

"I remember standing beside the hedge, gazing down at Charlie. His face was whiter than white; his hair a matted tangle of blood. I had always thought people died with their eyes shut, but Charlie's were wide open. He was staring at me, and I was staring at him. It was like looking into someone's soul. I wanted to turn away, but I couldn't. My body was seized up like the tin man in *The Wizard of Oz*. The meningitis must have really started to get the better of me.

"It felt like I stood there forever, but it couldn't have been more than a couple of minutes. I knew I should be doing something about Charlie, but I had no idea what, and it was hard to think over the jackhammer pounding in my head. It was survival instinct that finally got me moving. I couldn't let anybody see me there. So I bolted. The only thing I could think about was hiding. So I hurried back up Bone Tree Hill and climbed the tree.

"That's where I was when Mr. Gunderson showed up. He didn't waste a second getting to work. He hopped off the tractor, spread a brown plastic tarp on the ground, and proceeded to roll Charlie and the shovel up in it. After that, he tied the bundle with a rope and heaved it onto the tractor. You would have thought Charlie was a bag of seed instead of a human being, and my heart twisted inside my chest to watch him being thrown around like that."

"Then what happened?" Jilly asked breathlessly.

"I waited until the tractor was out of sight, then I climbed down from the tree and followed it. Once I got to the other side of the field, I crouched behind a bale of hay. I could see the tractor parked beside the cornfield, but there was no sign of Mr. Gunderson or Charlie. So I stayed where I was and waited.

"A couple of minutes later, Mr. Gunderson came out of the corn — alone. He headed straight for the tractor, started it up, and drove to the barn. The second he disappeared from view, I took off for the cornfield. I had to know where he'd taken Charlie. Every step was torture, but I tried to ignore the pain. I couldn't give up. I turned up the row I'd seen Mr. Gunderson exit, and about halfway along I found Charlie."

The scene was so vivid in my mind I don't know how I could have forgotten it. The brown tarpaulin dumped carelessly on the ground might have been an old carpet or a roll of tar paper. Not a person. Not Charlie! A sense of hopelessness and helplessness surged through me just as it had then.

"Oh, Jilly!" I didn't even try to keep the anguish out of my voice. "I didn't know what to do. I needed to get help, but I couldn't leave Charlie — not there — not like that. It . . . it . . . just wouldn't have been right." I searched her face for understanding.

She put a hand on my arm. "It must have been awful. No wonder you've blocked out the memory all these years."

It took a few seconds for Jilly's words to register. I had been trying so hard to remember that day, it was difficult to get my head around the idea that part of me was working just as hard to forget it. I had assumed my loss of memory was because of the fever, but maybe Jilly was right. Maybe I'd forgotten on purpose.

"So what did you do?" she said quietly.

I shook my head. "Nothing. It was like I was in a dream. I just sat there. But then I heard footsteps. Or maybe I felt the vibration of footsteps through the ground. It doesn't matter. The point is that someone was coming, and the prospect of getting caught scared me out of my daze. So I started scrambling through the rows of corn — like you and I did the other night — as quickly and quietly as I could. Then when I was far enough away that I didn't think anyone would see me, I threw myself onto the dirt.

"It was Mr. Gunderson, and he was carrying another shovel. He marched between the rows of corn and when he got to Charlie, he started to dig — not on the path, but in one of the rows. He carefully removed several plants, roots and all, and set them aside. Then he dug a big hole where they had been. Once it was deep enough, he rolled Charlie into it, covered him with dirt, and replaced the corn. When everything looked just like it had before, he left."

"That must have taken forever," Jilly said. "And you were lying on the ground the whole time?"

I shrugged. "I didn't really have a choice, and anyway the ground was cool, and I was burning up. But as soon as Mr. Gunderson was gone, I knew I had to get out of there. I had to tell my parents everything that had happened. I had to get help. I pushed through the remaining rows of corn and tore off across the hayfield. It wasn't until I was on top of Bone Tree Hill again that I finally stopped to look back. Mr. Gunderson was standing at the far side of the field, and he was looking straight at me."

Jilly gasped and covered her mouth.

"I was so scared," I said. "All I could think about was getting home. I'm pretty sure I flew the rest of the way."

"Did Mr. Gunderson chase you?"

I frowned. "I don't know. I don't remember anything after I started running. I don't even remember getting home, and obviously I never told my parents about Charlie, so I must have been pretty out of it."

"Wow," Jilly breathed softly. "That's horrible. I can't even imagine it. You were way braver than I would have been, Jess, especially considering you were so sick. And to think Mr. Gunderson had you in his clutches just yesterday. He could have killed you!"

I shuddered. "Don't remind me."

Jilly picked up the shovel and hefted it over her shoulder. "So now we go to the police."

I kicked a clod of earth. "I guess."

Jilly's jaw dropped open. "You *guess*? What do you mean, you *guess*? What's there to guess about? You know where the body is. You know where the murder weapon is. You tell the police, they dig up the cornfield, and Mr. Gunderson goes to jail. Case closed."

I shrugged. "Or maybe I do."

Jilly actually shoved me. "What is your problem?" she snarled. "You did *not* kill Charlie! Mr. Gunderson did. When are you going to get that through your head? All the evidence points to *him*."

I shook my head. "No, Jilly. You just think it does. The evidence can be interpreted other ways. You keep forgetting that I was there."

"But you didn't kill Charlie. And you don't remember anything! You said so yourself."

"But I know what I feel. As much as I want you to be right, I don't think you are. My gut says I'm the one who killed Charlie. I'm just praying that when the whole story finally comes out, we'll discover it was an accident or something. Otherwise I don't think I'll be able to live with myself. If I — "

"Stop it!" Jilly snapped, cutting me off. "Stop it right now. You didn't kill anyone. I know that in *my* gut. I say we go to the police right now with what you remember and let them handle this. They'll dig up the body and the shovel and arrest Mr. Gunderson. You'll see."

I stared hard at Jilly. "Maybe Charlie isn't there anymore."

"What are you talking about? Why wouldn't he be there?"

"All this happened six years ago," I said.

"So?"

"So maybe Mr. Gunderson moved the body. He knows I saw him bury it, so it would make sense to move it. And if he did, how would it look for the police to storm in there, tear up his garden, and find nothing? They'd think I was either a troublemaker or a nut case."

Jilly clucked her tongue. "They would not."

"They would," I insisted. "And then what's Mr. Gunderson going to do?"

Jilly didn't miss a beat. "Make good on his threat to kill you?"

"Jilly!" I wailed.

"Sorry," she apologized. "But you have to admit he'd get caught for that for sure."

"Thanks. That makes me feel so much better."

There was a long silence. It was Jilly who broke it. "So are we going to the police or not?"

I squinted toward the Gunderson farm and then looked back at Jilly. "Yes, I guess we have to. There isn't any other choice. This thing has to end. I can't take it anymore." I paused. "But I have to do something first."

"What?"

"I have to make sure Charlie is still in the cornfield."

Jilly's eyes narrowed suspiciously. "And exactly how do you propose to do that?"

I cocked one eyebrow. "There's really only one way, isn't there? I can't very well ask Mr. Gunderson, so my only option is to dig."

"Are you out of your friggin' mind?" Jilly bellowed as she jammed the shovel into the ground.

"Probably," I conceded. "But I've suspected that for quite a while, so I'm pretty much used to the idea. I have to do this, Jilly. Don't you see?"

"No," She shook her head vehemently. "No, I don't see. What you're talking about is way too dangerous."

"You think I don't know that? It's my arm Mr. Gunderson nearly broke, remember? I know the man is dangerous." Then I added, "That's why I'm not asking you to come with me."

"Well, you're sure as heck not going *without* me," she shot back. "And since I'm not going, neither are you."

Jilly and I stood there, arguing back and forth for another fifteen minutes, but it didn't do any good. Neither of us was giving an inch. Finally I said, "This isn't solving anything. All it's doing is making me hungry. Have you eaten yet?"

"Yeah," she said. "An hour ago. But I could probably force down a muffin or a piece of toast — to keep you company."

"Right," I rolled my eyes and grabbed her hand. "Come on. Let's go see what Gran's making for breakfast."

She pulled the shovel out of the ground and was about to swing it onto her shoulder, but I took it from her and leaned it against the tree.

"Just leave it here for now," I said.

Jilly jammed her hands onto her hips. "Jessica Lawler," she scolded me, "don't you even think about it."

"Think about what?" I feigned annoyance. "I just want to come back and clean up the mess I've made here. Honestly, Jilly. You have such a suspicious mind."

I was lying, of course, and we both knew it. I was going to need that shovel when I went to the cornfield later that night.

"All right, I'm dead curious. I don't deny it," Gran said as she set down a platter of blueberry pancakes and bacon in front of us. "What treasure could you possibly be searching for at six o'clock in the morning? Is this one of those radio show competitions where they hide something in the city and then give out clues until somebody finds it?"

Without realizing it, my grandmother had offered me the perfect explanation for my early morning expedition. All I had to say was 'yes' and I wouldn't have to deflect any more questions. It was very tempting. But it would also be lying, and Gran deserved better than that. Even so, I didn't want to tell her what I knew about Charlie's death and about Mr. Gunderson burying him in the cornfield. She'd drag me off to the police station before I could swallow what was in my mouth. The trick was going to be giving her enough information to satisfy her curiosity without telling her the whole story.

"Actually, Gran, the treasure I was hunting for was my memory," I said.

Jilly stopped spreading butter on her pancakes.

"When Jilly told me Charlie Castle had disappeared, it was a total surprise. I had no memory of that day. I guess that's because of the meningitis." I shrugged. "Anyway, since Charlie and I were on Bone Tree Hill the day he went missing, I thought that if I went up there and wandered around a bit, my memory might come back and I'd be able to tell the police something to help them locate Charlie." I shrugged again. "That's all."

Jilly resumed buttering.

Gran nodded. "I should have guessed as much. Since you've come to visit, you've been going up there almost as often as you did when you were a child. I suspected it wasn't just for old time's sake." She slid into a chair across from me and wrapped both hands around her coffee mug. "So has your theory proved correct?"

"Not yet," I sighed. "But I'm not giving up. I'll probably head back up there later today."

Beneath the table, Jilly kicked me.

Fifteen

Jilly and I argued on and off for most of the day. I was determined to visit the cornfield that evening, and she was just as determined to keep me away. Finally I'd had enough.

"For crying out loud," I said, throwing down the sponge I'd been using to wash my grandmother's car. It splatted onto the concrete driveway, shooting bullets of soapy water into the air and causing Jilly to jump away from the tire she'd been scrubbing. "Nothing you say is going to change my mind, so give it a rest. I don't want to discuss this anymore."

"Somebody has to try to talk some sense into you," she protested. "Unless you haven't noticed, you're not exactly thinking str — "

I picked up the hose, pointed it at her, and prepared to turn on the nozzle. "What part of 'I don't want to talk about this' didn't you understand?" I asked.

She held up her hands and put the car between us. "Fine. I get the message. Have it your way. Go and get yourself killed. See if I care. Just don't spray me with the hose. With the dirt you threw at me earlier, I'll turn into a mud pie."

A picture of Jilly covered from head to foot in gooey mud popped into my head. She looked like a chocolate Easter treat that had been left out in the sun, and because my nerves were jangled beyond rational thought, the image cracked me up and I crumpled to the pavement, laughing hysterically.

"Oh, Jilly," I gasped when I'd finally laughed myself out. "Thank you. You have no idea how much I needed that."

She beamed. "Well, you know me. Anything for a friend." Then she picked up the sponge I'd dropped, chucked it at me, and went back to scrubbing the tire. "Which brings me to the next subject. When are we going to the cornfield?"

Jilly thought we should wait until after dark, because there would be less chance of being seen. Though that was true, it created another problem — namely, we wouldn't be able to see where we were going. Without streetlights to illuminate our way, we'd be stumbling around like two blind mice. Even with the full moon, we'd be tripping over ourselves. We'd have to take flashlights, and anyone looking toward the cornfield was bound to spot the glow.

I suggested we head out around nine o'clock, since that's when Christina had said Mr. Gunderson closed the roadside stand for the night. If he was at the stand, he couldn't be near the cornfield. It would probably take him a half hour or so to pack up the produce and load it onto his truck and then another fifteen minutes to unload it at the other end. That would give Jilly and me around forty-five minutes of uninterrupted time to look for Charlie. It wasn't much, but if we dug fast it could work, especially since I had no intention of actually exhuming Charlie's body. I just wanted to go down far enough to reach him. Once I assured myself he was there, I would shovel the dirt back in place and head for the police.

By eight thirty, Jilly and I were on Bone Tree Hill. Since the work would go faster with two of us digging, we'd brought another shovel and were using it to repair the damage I'd inflicted earlier on the ground around the tree. Once we'd tidied the area as well as we could, we sat down and gazed across the valley toward the Gunderson farm, waiting for nine o'clock to arrive.

"I realize I've said this before," I sighed, "but it really is beautiful up here."

"Mmm-hmm," Jilly mumbled. "You have and it is."

"In a way, it's kind of weird. I know that when we were growing up we did lots of different things, but Bone Tree Hill is always what pops into my head when I think about being a kid."

Jilly leaned back on her elbows. "I know what you mean. It's like that for me too. I guess that's part of the reason I never wanted to come up here after you moved away."

"Bone Tree Hill." I said the words softly and let them float away on the evening breeze. Then I turned to Jilly and frowned. "Have we always called it that?"

She sent me a sideways glance. "You don't remember?"

"No." Then I rolled my eyes. "So what else is new, right?"

Jilly shook her head. "Nice try, but you can't use meningitis as an excuse for this one. It goes back to when we were seven. In those days it was my brothers who used to come up here — well, Denny and Glen anyway. Eddie was only four, so his big adventure was the backyard sandbox. Anyhow, this is where they hung out, and when they talked about the tree, the rope swing, and the forts they built, you and I used to get insanely jealous. We wanted to do all that stuff too. Personally, I think my brothers juiced up the stories just to egg us on. If you recall, we weren't even allowed to cross the road back then, so trekking up the hill was a definite no-no." She sniggered. "But we begged and begged, and finally our parents gave in.

We weren't allowed to go alone though. Denny and Glen had to escort us."

A light went on in my head. "Wait a second. I think I remember this now. On the walk up the trail, didn't they try to scare us with some creepy story about the tree?"

Jilly laughed and nodded. "Yeah. They said that a long time ago a cattle rustler had been lynched there and left to hang as an example to anyone else who might have thoughts about stealing cattle. The birds pecked at his body until his flesh fell off and all that was left were his bones. Over time, most of those broke off too and were gnawed to nothing by man-eating dogs, but the rest were still in the tree." She laughed again.

"And we actually believed that?"

"Hey, we were seven-years old!" she said. "Besides the guys had proof. Way up in the tree, they'd hung some bones — no doubt the remains of a chicken dinner, but you and I were too little to know that then — so we were scared out of our minds. I think we screamed the whole way home. We probably *never* would have gone back if I hadn't overheard Denny and Glen bragging to a couple of their friends a few days later about how they'd tricked us."

"The little brats!" I exclaimed. "I sure hope you paid them back."

Jilly grinned. "I'm sure I must have. It isn't like me to let a crime like that go unpunished. I probably stuffed the fingers of their baseball gloves with peanut butter or something."

We both chuckled.

"Anyway," Jilly added, "once you and I started hanging out on the hill, the boys stopped coming. So in the end, we were the winners." Then she glanced at her watch and her expression sobered. "It's time."

There was no sense trying to act nonchalant with shovels in our hands, so we tore down the hill to the hedge and took cover. Then — when we were sure there was no one nearby — we jumped the fence and ran across the hayfield.

It was actually a bit spooky. The hay had been newly bailed, just like the day Charlie had been murdered, and I glanced around nervously, half-expecting to see the tractor. But it wasn't there. Hopefully that meant Mr. Gunderson had finished his work for the day and wouldn't be back. The tightness in my chest eased a little.

We lay on our stomachs at the edge of the hayfield, peering toward the farm. When we were sure the coast was clear, we hurried down the slope to the cornfield and slipped in the back. That meant squeezing through the rows instead of walking between them. It was a lot more work but it kept us hidden, so it was worth it.

The cornfield was huge, but I moved without hesitation, pushing my way confidently between the plants. It was as if I was being pulled to Charlie by a magnet.

"Are you sure this is the spot?" Jilly whispered anxiously when I came to a stop.

I nodded. "I'm positive. How much time do we have?"

Jilly checked her watch. "It's ten past nine. That gives us about half an hour."

"Okay," I said, and pointed to the ground. "You dig here — straight down. All we're trying to do is make contact with the tarp. Once we know it's there, we'll replace the dirt and get the heck out of here." I moved a few steps away. "I'll start here."

We didn't speak again. We were too busy digging. After twenty minutes, I started to panic. We were both down a good three feet, but there was still no sign of Charlie — and we were running out of time. Maybe I had picked the wrong spot, or maybe Mr. Gunderson had moved the body. All I knew was that if we didn't find something soon, we were going to have to give up. We couldn't take the chance of being caught.

And then, "I've got something!" Jilly whispered excitedly. "It's brown. And it's plastic. It's got to be Charlie! You were right. He's here. We've found him!"

"That's unfortunate," a voice behind us said quietly, causing Jilly and I to spin around so fast we bumped into each another.

"You should have paid attention to my husband's warning." Mrs. Gunderson shook her head sadly, and I noted that she looked very much like she had the evening she'd caught us in the barn — right down to the apron. The only difference was that this time she was wielding a machete instead of a broom. Neither Jilly nor I could take our eyes off it. For several seconds the three of us stood perfectly still, frozen in the moment. It was Mrs. Gunderson who broke the spell. To my horror, she took a step toward us and raised the machete.

As she did, blinding orange and white sparks flashed inside my head, and I winced. But as suddenly as they had come, they were gone, and all that was left was a sickening vision.

I blinked incredulously at Mrs. Gunderson.

"Oh, my god," I said. "It was you."

Sixteen

Suddenly I was facing the whole horrible nightmare all over again.

I opened my eyes gingerly and squinted up at the evening sky. It felt like someone had jabbed a thousand needles into my eyeballs. But that was nothing compared to the fifty thousand drums beating inside my head. My stomach began to roll. The last thing I needed was to throw up, so I pushed the prospect from my mind and concentrated all my thoughts on the tall grass surrounding me. The sun-bleached stalks waved lazily in the breeze, tickling my arms and legs. I could see them, but I couldn't feel them, and that's when I realized I was sick. I tried to lift my head, but the effort was excruciating and made me break into a sweat.

I lay back down and tried to think. I was on Bone Tree Hill — that much I knew. And clearly I was alone. But how had I gotten here? At first I drew a blank. There was nothing in my head except pain. And then from the shadows a faint image of Amanda floated through the thick fog in my mind. She was headed down the trail — away from the hill — and she was running as if the Devil himself was chasing her.

That's when I heard the voices. At first I couldn't tell if they were real or if I was imagining them. I lay very still and listened.

They seemed to be coming from behind me on the Gunderson farm side of Bone Tree Hill.

I took a few deep breaths and eased myself over onto my stomach. Then resting my chin on my arms I peered through the long grass toward the sound. There were two people — Charlie and someone else — and they were arguing. I didn't recognize the other person right away, probably because I'd only ever seen Mrs. Gunderson at the roadside stand, and without the bins of fruit and vegetables around her, I couldn't place her face.

Mrs. Gunderson was doing most of the talking — yelling actually. She was obviously angry about something.

"Where is it!" she screeched over and over again. "I know you took it, and I want it back." She shook her head scornfully. "Right from the beginning I could tell you were going to be trouble. I told Nils you were a bad one. But he wouldn't listen. Well, I was right, wasn't I? You are nothing but a lying little thief! Now give me that box!"

"No!" Charlie bellowed, pushing her away and striding toward the hedge. "I don't have it anymore."

Mrs. Gunderson clutched at him, but he twisted free.

"What have you done with it?" she demanded. "I want it back."

Charlie threw down the shovel he'd been carrying and rounded on her so suddenly, she fell back a few steps. "Why?" he roared. "You never used the stupid box anyway. All it did was sit in a cupboard. I needed it, so I took it," he finished defiantly.

Charlie was the same height as Mrs. Gunderson and a lot heavier, but she wasn't cowed by his size. She grabbed a handful of his shirt and tugged on it, pulling him close. "Where is it! Give it to me right this minute or I'll — "

"Or you'll what?" Charlie interrupted her. He was still yelling, but his voice was shaking now. "Or you'll send me back to family services? Who cares? I wish you would. It couldn't be worse than here. At least there they don't call you names or snoop in your stuff. At least there — "

Charlie's rant was cut short by a slap across his face.

"You ungrateful little monster!" she growled. "You don't even have the brains you were born with. Why, if it weren't for Nils and me you would be rotting in that place. Nobody wants a crazy half-wit like you." She laughed cruelly. "Look at you. Your own parents don't even want you."

Charlie's face flushed almost purple and he started to cry. "They do so!" he said in a strangled voice. "They do so. They just can't look after me right now. You don't know anything."

He was so upset I wanted to call out to him, to comfort him.

Mrs. Gunderson, however, was unmoved. "Look at you," she sneered again, "crying like a little girl. You're disgusting." Then she got into his face again. "I'm warning you for the last time. Give me the box!"

Charlie swiped at the tears on his cheeks, then bent down and scooped up the shovel. I thought Mrs. Gunderson's badgering had finally gotten to him, and he was giving in. But to my surprise he pushed the shovel into her hands and said, "Find it yourself."

Then he turned and started toward the hedge once more.

"Don't you walk away when I'm talking to you," she shrieked.

Charlie ignored her.

Beside herself with rage, Mrs. Gunderson took off after him, screeching the whole time. But Charlie might as well have been deaf — he just kept going. Since she was running and he was walking, it didn't take her long to catch up, and when she did, she hauled the shovel back and swung it with all her might. It happened so fast that I didn't have a chance to warn Charlie.

Even from my hiding place on the hill, I heard the sound of metal striking bone. It was sickening.

Charlie didn't cry out. He didn't turn around either. All he did was crumple to the ground as if his bones had suddenly dissolved. For a minute, Mrs. Gunderson just stared at him. She didn't touch him or bend down to see if he was all right. She just stared. Finally she started running for the farm, and I knew Charlie was dead.

That's when I threw up.

When there was nothing left in my stomach, I forced myself to stand. The world spun a little at first, but eventually it slowed down, and I stumbled down the hill to Charlie.

"It was you," I said again, staring with disbelief at Mrs. Gunderson. "You killed Charlie."

Mrs. Gunderson stopped walking and lowered the machete — a little. "So you *did* see me that evening." She didn't try to deny my accusation. She just shrugged. "We didn't know. Nils thought you'd seen him bury the body, but that was all." Her expression became puzzled. "So why didn't you tell? If you knew, why didn't you tell?"

Considering the way she was waving the machete around, I should have been afraid. But I wasn't. Or maybe I was, and shock had given me a false sense of calm. The situation was too unreal to get my head around. Though Mrs. Gunderson was standing only a few feet away, holding the largest, sharpest, knife I'd ever seen, she didn't seem like a murderer. She was certainly nothing like the crazed woman I had seen kill Charlie.

I opened my mouth to say I hadn't reported the murder because I hadn't remembered it before now, but Jilly spoke first.

"She *did* tell," she blurted. Her voice was a bit shaky, but considering the situation, it was understandable. "The police know all about what you did. In fact, they're on their way right now. We're supposed to meet them here."

Jilly's words caught Mrs. Gunderson off guard. She looked unsure, as if she were trying to decide if Jilly was telling the truth. Finally her face cleared, and she said, "You're lying. You're just trying to trick me."

"Suit yourself," Jilly shrugged, continuing to play out her bluff. "It's your funeral."

Inwardly I cringed. We were being held at knifepoint, and Jilly was still making puns.

"Why did you do it?" I said, trying to keep Mrs. Gunderson talking. "Why did you kill Charlie? He was just a kid."

Her expression instantly hardened, reminding me of the woman I'd seen arguing in the field.

"He was a thief." Her eyes flashed as she spat out the words. "He stole from me."

"It was a tin box." I forced myself to speak calmly, rationally. I didn't want to make Mrs. Gunderson angry.

But it appeared I already had.

"That box has been in my family for centuries!" she snapped. "It is a family heirloom, and that boy stole it."

I couldn't imagine Charlie caring about heirlooms even if he'd understood what they were. Perhaps he had taken the box because he'd known its loss would upset Mrs. Gunderson. If she'd been mean to him on a regular basis, the box might have been his way of getting even.

"Was it worth killing for?" I asked. I knew it was the wrong thing to say, but the question slipped out anyway.

Faster than I could blink, Mrs. Gunderson swung the machete, slicing a nearby corn plant cleanly in two. Jilly let out an involuntary gasp, and I jumped. We found each other's hands and held on tightly.

"I guess that answers that question," Jilly hissed into my ear.

I glanced quickly at the shovel near my feet. I considered making a dive for it, but Mrs. Gunderson was less than a body's length away. She could lop off my arm before I even touched the handle. Besides, I needed to hear what she had to say. After living with the horror of killing Charlie for so many months, I needed to know the real reason he had died.

Jilly cleared her throat. "So what are you going to do now?"

Mrs. Gunderson took her time answering. She seemed to be admiring the blade of the machete. "You haven't really left me a choice," she replied, and there was no doubt in my mind what she meant.

"You can't be serious," I said, hoping she might respond to logic. "You won't get away with it. The police will catch you."

"Mrs. Gunderson took another step toward us. "I don't see why." She spread her arms. "It's a big cornfield."

That's when I knew we were going to die. The woman was deranged. She had killed before and gotten away with it. She truly thought she could do it again, and nothing Jilly and I said or did was going to change her mind. The fact that she would most certainly be caught afterwards wasn't a consolation.

Mrs. Gunderson took another step in our direction.

Keeping my eyes peeled on the machete, I tried to back up. But I was already pressed up tight to the row of corn, and the heel of my runner caught on one of the plants. I lost my balance and stumbled. Jilly and I were still holding hands, so I jerked her with me, and the next thing I knew we were heading for the ground.

Mrs. Gunderson took another step and raised the machete.

"Mud pies!" I screamed at Jilly.

Another person might not have known what I was talking about — and there certainly wasn't time to explain — but Jilly and I have been friends a long time. Without hesitating, she scooped up a handful of dirt and threw it in Mrs. Gunderson's face. It struck her at exactly the same instant mine did.

Mrs. Gunderson staggered, swiping at the dirt in her eyes. Jilly and I tried to roll out of her way, but — blind or not — she was still swinging the machete, and it came so close to my ear I felt the blade stir the air.

Then she opened her eyes and, with a victorious sneer, once again raised the machete high above her head.

"Mia!" a man's voice bellowed.

Surprised, Mrs. Gunderson hesitated for just a split second, but it was long enough. I don't know where he came from, but suddenly Mr. Gunderson was behind his wife and he had hold of her wrist. He was trying to wrestle the machete away from her. But she was stronger than she looked, and she writhed frantically to free herself. All the while the machete was dancing dangerously in the air. Jilly and I huddled together and covered our heads.

"Nils!" Mrs. Gunderson cried. "Let me go. They know. They will tell. I have to stop them."

"No, Mia," Mr. Gunderson grunted as he continued to grapple with his wife for the knife. "No more killing."

Mrs. Gunderson wasn't giving up. With her free arm, she elbowed him hard in the stomach. The air gushed out of him and his knees gave out a little, but he continued to hang on to his wife's wrist.

"Mia. Stop," he gulped for air. "Let it be over. Please." The way he was pleading, I seriously began to think he was going to lose the battle, and then we'd all die.

"I have no choice!" Mrs. Gunderson screamed, fighting as hard as ever.

"Nor do I," he murmured. "I am sorry, my love," and with a single powerful jerk of his hand, he twisted her arm in its socket.

Bone snapped. Mrs. Gunderson screamed. And the machete tumbled to the ground.

Seventeen

As soon as Mr. Gunderson got the machete away from his wife, everything about him changed. Suddenly his only concern was the fact that she was hurt. Mrs. Gunderson had passed out from the pain, and the farmer now sat on the path between the rows of corn, stroking her hair, and talking to her softly in what I guessed was Swedish. It didn't seem to matter that she couldn't hear him. As for Jilly and me, we might as well have been invisible.

"We need to call an ambulance," Jilly said, whipping a cell phone from the pocket of her jeans.

I blinked in disbelief. "You've had your cell phone this whole time?"

She shot me a disdainful glare. "It's not like I had a chance to use it." Then she punched in 911 and within minutes, the Gunderson farm was crawling with emergency vehicles — ambulance, police cars — even a fire truck! There were uniforms everywhere.

The medical team dealt with Mrs. Gunderson immediately, checking the extent of her injuries, making her as comfortable as they could, and then whisking her off to the hospital. Jilly and I even got the once over, but the paramedics decided we were unhurt, which was fine with me; after our close encounter with Mrs. Gunderson, the last thing I wanted was to be stuck in a confined space with her.

Mr. Gunderson wanted to ride with his wife, but the police said they needed to ask him some questions, and as soon as the ambulance left, they escorted him into the house. When he emerged an hour later, he was in handcuffs. An officer put him in the back seat of a cruiser and then drove off — to the police station I guess. I didn't have a lot of time to think about it, because Jilly and I were busy answering questions ourselves.

I'm not sure, but I think it was the firefighters who dug up Charlie's body. I didn't stand around to watch. I couldn't. I just showed them where Charlie was buried and went back to wait with Jilly. I didn't even look when they took him away.

It was several hours before we were allowed to leave, and by then it was dark. Gran arrived just about the same time as the news team from the television station. I had phoned her so she wouldn't worry, but my call seemed to have had exactly the opposite effect. She was on the scene in a matter of minutes, ducking under the yellow crime tape and hurrying over to Jilly and me.

I won't pretend I wasn't glad to see her. Shock was finally starting to set in — or wear off — I'm not sure how that works. All I know is that everything was starting to catch up to me. I was shivering and my legs had turned to cooked spaghetti.

"You poor things," Gran cooed, pulling Jilly and me into a big hug. It would seem Jilly wasn't in any better shape than I was. "Let's get you girls home."

"I don't think the police are finished with us yet," Jilly said. Her voice was shaking.

"We'll see about that," Gran replied with a take-charge *harrumph*. "You two wait here. I'll be right back."

Sure enough — not five minutes later she returned, carrying a couple of blankets and towing a police officer behind her. He shepherded us through the mob of reporters to the safety of Gran's car.

Though it was a relief to have my nightmare over with, the days that followed were anything but restful. For starters, Jilly and I had to go to the police station to make a formal statement. We weren't going to have to testify in court though — thank goodness. Mr. and Mrs. Gunderson had both confessed to their parts in Charlie's death, which meant there would be no trial — just a hearing where the judge would pass sentence.

On the home front, life was plain crazy. My parents totally flipped when they found out what had happened, and it took Gran a good hour of talking to convince them they didn't need to fly out on the next plane to rescue me. Bryan wasn't much better, except he was hurt that I hadn't shared events with him as they were unfolding. As for Gran, she barely let me go to the bathroom by myself for the next two days. Jilly stayed close to home too, and the few times she did venture out, it was with a three-brother escort. I guess you could say we were all pretty spooked.

There was still one day left before I headed back to Calgary, but in my mind I was already there. I was anxious to see Bryan — my parents too, of course — and I was already gearing up for the start of classes at university.

I wanted to put this episode of my life behind me. I was ready to move on — almost. There was just one more thing I needed to do.

Constable Barnes was every bit as nice on the telephone as
he had been in person, and when I explained what I wanted,
he invited me to come to the station that afternoon. He was
waiting for me in the front hallway when I arrived and led me
to the same room he'd taken me to when I'd been to the station
to ask about Amanda.

"You've had quite the adventure," he said, sliding into a chair
across from me. "How are you feeling?"

"Better now," I smiled, "but it's not an experience I'd like to
have again, thank you."

"You should never have tried to solve this on your own,"
he frowned. "You almost got yourself killed — you *and* your
friend."

I could feel my cheeks heating up. "I know," I replied
sheepishly. "I didn't mean for things to go the way they did.
I intended to tell you what I knew. Honest. I just wanted to
make sure Charlie was still in the cornfield. I had buried the
memory — " I winced. I was getting as bad as Jilly with the
puns. "What I mean to say is I'd forgotten what had happened
to Charlie for so long that I wasn't sure my mind wasn't still
playing tricks on me. I didn't want to send you on a wild goose
chase."

He sighed and shook his head. "It wouldn't be the first time.
Besides, that's my job."

I nodded. "Sorry."

He patted my hand. "It's okay. Just remember for next
time."

"Next time!" I exclaimed. "There better not be a next
time."

We both laughed.

"Constable Barnes," I said, "what's going to happen to the
Gundersons?"

He shrugged. "I can't say for sure. That's up to the judge. But considering the circumstances, I'd say Nils Gunderson is looking at some jail time as an accessory after the fact. He didn't kill your friend, but he did cover up the murder. As for his wife," he sighed, "she's currently undergoing psychiatric tests. I'd say there's a pretty good chance she'll end up in a mental health facility for a while."

I nodded again. Despite everything that had happened, I felt sorry for the Gundersons. Mrs. Gunderson was clearly mentally unstable, and Mr. Gunderson had just been trying to protect her. What he had done was wrong, but I could understand why he'd done it. Besides, he'd saved my life.

"So," Constables Barnes made a big show of placing the tin box in front of me. It had been sitting to one side of the table during our conversation, and it had taken all my willpower not to stare at it. "This is what you've come to see."

"Yes." My voice was barely a whisper.

"Well, I'll leave you to it, then," he said, pushing back his chair. "I'll be down the hall. Let me know when you're finished."

For several minutes, I simply stared at the box. It was amazingly ordinary — grey tin with a delicate floral border etched in black. It was about twice the size of a recipe box and it had a hinged lid. There wasn't even a latch. Was this what Charlie had been killed for?

I picked it up. It was heavier than I'd expected. I tipped it to one side. Something slid along the bottom and bumped the inner wall. The box wasn't empty.

I placed it back onto the table and lifted the lid. There were a number of objects inside, but the first thing my eyes were drawn to made me catch my breath. It was the snow globe — the one I had given Charlie on his birthday all those years ago. He'd kept it.

My gaze moved on to a photograph in a fake gold frame. It was lying face down, and when I turned it over, I was momentarily taken aback. I had expected to see a picture of Charlie's parents or perhaps a dog he'd had when he was a little boy, but there was nothing like that. The photo was the one that would have come with the frame — a happy little generic family — mother, father and little boy, all smiling for the camera, complete with the name of the company that had manufactured the frame.

The next thing I noticed was a rock. It shouldn't have meant anything to me, but it did. I had tripped over that very rock while Jilly, Amanda, Charlie, and I had been playing up on Bone Tree Hill the spring before Charlie died. I remember tossing the rock to him.

"Hey," I'd said. "It's a heart, Charlie. Happy Valentine's Day."

I rolled the rock around in my hands. It was slippery smooth. Then I turned it over. 'CC Loves JL' was scratched into the stone. Something sharp and painful caught in my throat. I put the rock down.

There was one more thing in the box — a paper that had been folded and unfolded so many times, it barely held together. I opened it carefully and flattened it out. That's when the tears came, and before I could stop them, they splattered onto the page.

The paper was a cigarette ad torn from a magazine. It was nothing and everything all at once. In it, a handsome smiling man with a cigarette in his hand was sitting on a tree stump in front of a log cabin. It was Charlie's dad — at least Charlie's dad the way Charlie saw him.

"Oh, God!" A sob erupted from me before I could stop it. I covered my face and turned away. How had we all done this to him? Charlie hadn't been stealing the box to hurt Mrs. Gunderson. He had just needed a place to put the things that were important to him.

And for that he had died.

I don't know how long I cried, but eventually I let myself out of the room and went looking for Constable Barnes.

"Did the box tell you what you needed to know?" he asked.

I nodded. And then in a rush I said, "Constable Barnes, what's going to happen to Charlie's things. They won't get thrown away, will they?"

He must have seen how important his answer was because he put a reassuring hand on my arm and said, "No, Jessica. They won't get thrown away. They'll be given to his next of kin. Charlie's mother is dead. She was a drug addict and overdosed on heroin shortly after Charlie disappeared. But his dad lives up island, just outside Cowichan — some sort of a mountain man, I understand — right down to the log cabin. Charlie's remains and his belongings will be forwarded there."

It was as if a great burden had been lifted from me. Charlie was going to get to his father's log cabin after all.

"You make sure you email and telephone," Jilly said as she waved me through the departure gate at the airport. "We are not going to lose touch."

I rolled my eyes. "As if! Jilly Carlisle, you and I will be friends beyond the end of time, and you know it. But," I added, "it's your turn to visit me. Come to Calgary and bring Myles with you. We can double-date."

"Myles Robinson is not my boyfriend!" she declared vehemently. "How many times do I have to tell you that?"

"Until you die," I called back, "or until your silver wedding anniversary. Whatever comes first. In the meantime, trust me. The guy has the hots for you. I know about this stuff."

I waved until she disappeared from view.

Then I made my way to the passenger lounge and boarded the plane. It was full, except for one empty seat — the one beside mine. But then it wasn't really empty. Charlie was in it. He flew all the way back to Calgary with me.

Teacher turned author, Kristin Butcher's professional writing career began in 1997 with the publication of her novel, *The Runaways*. Fourteen more books have since followed including CLA honour book, *The Gramma War* (Orca Book Publishers), and Chocolate Lily Award winning *Zee's Way* (Orca Book Publishers). Whether she's writing for a younger audience or for teens, Butcher is totally devoted to drawing her readers into her books so that they become a part of the story. Butcher lives in Campbell River, British Columbia.